COLBY

A BROKEN HORN RANCH NOVEL

R.M. NEILL

Cover by: Cate Ashwood Designs

Edited by: Jen Sharon Fiction Editing and Proofreading

Proofreading: Sarah Coppin

This is one is for you, Mom.
I love you.

Before We Begin

This book is set in Canada. There may be a few terms you don't recognize if you've never lived here. Being Canadian, it's what I know, so it's also what I write.

I consulted with a member of our provincial law enforcement on legal matters for this book. To make some story elements play out like I wanted, I bent the rules a smidge. I think it's still close enough to remain believable, but if you disagree, it's a choice I made for the story and entirely my creative decision.

Prologue

Colby

Five years earlier

My feet hit the floor of the barn with a muffled thump when I dismount from my horse. The dull barn lights throw more shadows than light, and I search the dark corners for Dante.

"Babe, do you see him in here, girl?"

She swishes her tail with a low whinny as I uncinch her saddle and slide it off. Placing the saddle on its stand, I feed Babe her carrot and continue to scan the barn for Dante. He knows I ride every Wednesday evening. My mom works late tonight, so we don't have to hurry inside for supper either. My stepdad, Brian, doesn't really keep track of us, and that suits me just fine.

Ever since mom met Brian and moved him and his son in with us, my world has been turned around. My mom smiles more, and she's not so stressed out about paying all the bills. I do what I can to help around the house and make it easier, but money creates just as many problems as it solves. Until Brian showed up, the expense of a horse was next on the list to be cut, but I wouldn't allow my mom to do it. When my dad died, Babe was still new to me and she was a comfort I needed. Without her, grieving would have been so much harder. There was no way I'd give up this horse without a fight.

I didn't care much for Brian, but he made our lives easier in the money and paying bills situation. But more difficult in other areas. Specifically with his son, Dante.

My new stepbrother had little to say initially, and it wasn't just because he was shy. Once we finally started talking and spending time together, he opened up to me, in more ways than one. We had a lot in common and one of those things was a mutual attraction we didn't know what to do with at first.

Strong, capable hands land on my butt cheeks and a small yelp crosses my lips.

"Good grief! You scared the shit out of me!"

My heart races from the scare, but also from the boy himself. Turning around, I loop my arms around Dante's neck as he dips his head and peppers kisses up mine.

"Sorry, Colbs. Your ass always looks good in these jeans." His hands slide down to squeeze my cheeks. "I just had to go for it, you know?"

"Help me with Babe first, then you can *go* for whatever you like."

I steal a final kiss and push him away playfully. With knowing glances we work together to replenish Babe's water and feed so we can have as much time together as possible. It's not often we spend extended periods in private.

"I can't wait until we're off to college. I hate only sneaking around with you," he says while he fills the water trough for my horse.

He's so cute when he's put off about something and it only makes my heart swell to know he's looking forward to the two of us not hiding anymore. Not that either of us is ashamed of loving each other. The pressure of being stepbrothers is what has us keeping to ourselves.

"Graduation is next week. We'll both be nineteen soon. Then it's another six weeks until we move to the student housing." I hang my Stetson on the hook outside Babe's stall and hook a finger through his belt loop. With a tug, he steps into me, hands already sneaking under my shirt, greedy to touch me everywhere he can.

"It's so long, though." He presses his forehead to mine with a sigh.

Not as long as if I had to live forever without you.

"I know, but we'll be busy working and it'll pass quickly."

He crashes his mouth into mine and steals my breath as we stumble together out of Babe's stall and onto the hay bales stacked in the corner.

"I want to taste you, Colbs, please."

My strangled groan of consent barely leaves my lips and Dante drops to his knees. I brace myself against the hay bales as he tugs my pants down to free my dick. There's zero finesse today. It's all teenage hormones and instant gratification, and I'm okay with that. In a few months we'll have all the lazy Sundays, couch snuggles and tender moments I could ever want. But until then, I'll take this.

Dante wastes no time and engulfs as much of me as he can at once. I gasp at the sensation of his warm mouth and the slide of his tongue. He fumbles with his own pants in a frantic effort to touch himself. When he finally has himself in hand, he moans around my cock and my hips thrust forward.

Dante gags and peers up at me from under his beautiful, dark eyelashes. His hand moves lightning fast as he jerks himself off and I thrust into his mouth again.

"You're so hot like that." My voice is hoarse as I cup his cheek and thrust again, "I'm not gonna last long."

I'd normally be embarrassed at how fast my orgasm comes crashing into me, but I've been thinking about this all day and Dante doing anything with his mouth pushes all my hot buttons.

"Oh, fuck." I push his head away and stumble back as I come in my hand. Dante stays on his knees and offers his open mouth and tongue to me.

I'm so lucky he's mine.

Stepping closer, I allow him to lap at the sticky mess and when he does, I need to bite my lip to keep quiet. He drops his forehead to my hip and spills into his hand with a muttered curse.

Our ragged breaths float through the silence of the barn. My heart tries to calm itself down, but it's jumping into my mouth as I peer down my body and drink in this beautiful boy at my feet. I could never love anyone more than him.

"I could do this every day and twice on Sundays," Dante mumbles as he staggers to his feet.

Laughing, I press a kiss to his lips. "Soon, D. Very soon we will."

The icy cold barn tap water is fine for hand wash ups, but not so much for the other body parts. We manage to remove the traces of sex and spend more time kissing in the hay, because it's never enough with him. At first, I thought it was just me being a horny teenager. But it's so much more than just seeking ways to get off.

Dante is in all my life plans. He fills the void like no one else can. My friend, my protector, my cheerleader and my true love. Without him, well, I don't even want to go back to life without him. Fuck the people who might give us a hard time because our parents are married to each other.

Finally leaving the barn, we stroll towards the house holding hands and stealing kisses like any normal couple would. While I tell him it's not much longer until we leave for college, it feels like an eternity. But I refuse to let him be down about it.

When we draw closer to the house, the motion light shines and Brian, Dante's dad, steps back into the house. Dante's hand drops mine and he steps away. I miss his closeness immediately.

"He wasn't supposed to be home until later." His whisper is pained, and even in the low glow of the outdoor light, I notice his body tense.

"He didn't see anything. Don't panic, D. We were out with Babe, that's all."

Dante nods, but his whole body is stiff and robotic. The tick in his jaw is the only movement that seems natural.

Inside the house, Brian isn't in any of the common areas and some of the tension Dante's holding seeps away.

"I'm just going to go to my room and study for tomorrow. I'll catch you in the morning, Colby."

He brushes his fingertips lightly down my back before moving past me.

Dante's broad back walking to his bedroom is the last part of him I see.

When I wake up the next morning, he's gone.

Chapter 1

Dante

Present Day

T hree years ago I made a mistake.

Today is the day I hope to get my life back. Or at least start to.

The guard on the holding cell side gives me a final pat down. I've been through so many searches today my dick is starting to think it's foreplay. The buzzer sounds, and the door unlocks leading me into the discharge area. It's still a secured area, but the cells have been left behind. It's one step closer to the outside and, with a bit of luck, the life I left behind.

"Here's your bus pass and a route map." The barked orders from the guard behind the plexi glass draw my attention and I step closer. "You'll get dropped off at the closest bus stop from the facility at the time you choose. Just let the shuttle driver know when you want to be there."

Facility. That's what they call it. Not a prison or an institution, but a facility. Like it has any other purpose aside from housing prisoners until their time is served. It certainly had no other purpose for me, unless you count reminding me every day there was quite likely nothing for me to go back to.

I jam the bus pass and map into my jeans pocket and the cardboard pass pokes me through the thin pocket liner.

"As soon as I can get there would be preferable." I try to keep the contempt from my voice. I really do. But this jail guard is riding high on the superiority complex today, and I just want to get the fuck out of here.

"You might want to mind your manners, son." He pushes a plastic bag through the slot to me. My only personal possessions in the whole world. The prick of tears threaten, but I blink them back and snatch my plastic bag of memories before the guard changes his mind.

"Sorry." I mumble and keep my eyes trained on the floor.

He slides an envelope through the window next. "The balance of your commissary, wages and anything someone deposited for you is in this envelope. There's an address for a halfway house and a soup kitchen as well. Since you're not being released to family, I'll assume you may need those."

Thanks for the reminder, asshole.

"Your probation officer will expect you on Tuesday. Don't be late and they'll help you with anything else you need. Any questions?"

I'm still trying to grapple with the fact that in a few hours I'll be sleeping in a shelter and likely eating at a soup kitchen. The questions I do want to ask, he can't answer.

"No, sir." My respectful tone has returned. I just need to keep it together a little longer and I'll be out of this concrete cube. I've followed all the rules for three years, now is not the time to break any.

The buzzer sounds, sliding the next door open, and I step into the hallway. I'm officially no longer behind bars and my heart pounds. The same sun that shines within the prison yard feels brighter out here, passing through windows without bars in hopeful greeting.

Another guard, this one friendlier, greets me. "Big day. I'll escort you to the shuttle. I assume no one is here to pick you up?"

He doesn't mean to sound cruel. I notice the flinch after the words leave his mouth. But he's right. In three years, nobody came to visit. Nobody called.

Because nobody knew where I was. Especially not the one person I wanted to see the most.

"You assume right."

With a nod, he leads the way, rubber soled shoes squeaking on the polished floors. My stomach flips as we near the entrance, and the shuttle waits outside. Through the glass doors, giant letters spell *prison transport* across the side of the shuttle. There's no way people don't know who's inside. The shuttle is its own kind of twisted scarlet letter and it's the last ride I'll ever take in one.

"Here's your ride. You have a good day now. And I hope I don't see you back here."

His joke falls flat, but he means well, and I nod his way to acknowledge him. His footsteps fade away and I'm left with the spring breeze ruffling my hair and a crinkly plastic bag under my arm.

My feet stay frozen, eyes locked on the shuttle – *the prisoner transport* - remembering the night I was thrown into it and taken here. Snot and tears stained my face, and I wanted to throw up, but couldn't since I hadn't eaten for two days prior. But this time, it's taking me away from here. I'm getting out, but my legs are concrete pillars.

"Hey! Am I taking you somewhere or not?"

The driver is the same pasty faced overweight man I remember from that first night. He gave no fucks about me or my problem. He didn't care that some guy with his whole life ahead of him was just sentenced for a crime he wanted no part of. I was guilty due to ignorance, and that was my own fault.

Tilting my head back to view the partly overcast skies, I sigh. It's sunny now, but those are rain clouds. If I don't take this ride, I'll not only be soaked to the bone, but I'll have to walk at least thirty kilometers to the bus stop.

I clear my throat. "Yes, please."

He opens the back door of the van and I swallow back the bile while taking a place on the bench seat. The door slams behind me and sweat beads on my forehead.

It's only thirty kilometers. I can do this.

"Do you want the bus stop, or do you have a specific place to go?"

The engine rumbles under my feet and my nails bite into my palms as he maneuvers the van through the prison yard and out the secured gates. I can't even have the pleasure of seeing the prison disappear behind me. I only know we're through the gates because I hear the same metallic clunk as I did on the night I first came here.

The guard's voice comes over the intercom, all static filled and robotic.

"I can drop you at the bus stop or the courthouse in town. Those are your only options." There's a pause and he adds, "The courthouse is close to a shelter if you need a place to go tonight."

Does everyone need to remind me today I have nowhere to go?

As much as I hate to accept his offer, I know I need a place to stay.

"The courthouse, please."

He acknowledges me and I'm left to myself, the tires humming along on the pavement my only sound. I shift on the hard bench and crack open the envelope to see how much money I have to my name. Three hundred and twenty-five dollars, that's it. That's all I know I have with certainty.

I still have the plastic bag with my personal belongings tucked under my arm. It's clear, no privacy for the contents, just like behind the prison walls. My fingers itch to go through it all and find the one thing I treasured the most before my life went sideways. But I'm not looking yet. Not here.

The van rolls to a stop and the back doors open. With shaking legs, I lurch to the back and step down, mumbling a thank you to the driver before blindly following the sidewalk. For the first time in years, I can do what I want, and while I've wished for it for so long, I'm scared as hell.

I know this town. Well, I used to. A lot has changed.

After several blocks, I spot a secondhand clothing store and slip inside. I hope I smile warmly at the clerk. She doesn't cringe, so it must be a passable smile.

"Can I help you with anything?"

Her voice is laced with kindness, and my body immediately relaxes. I miss that tone, a genuine concern for my well being.

"I could use some help. I, um, I need a backpack I guess, and uh, clothes?"

The fucking tears threaten again and my nose tingles, but I'm not going there. Not even when her warm hand rests on my arm.

"Come over here, love. We'll get you all set up, okay? Don't even worry about a thing."

Nodding, I let her lead me to a chair where I sit without being asked, and she motions to a mini fridge.

"Help yourself. If you need a snack or something there's lots to choose from. I'll find some clothes you might like. What size do you think you are?"

She studies my frame and there's no contempt for the tattoos on my arm or the piercing on my eyebrow. She sees me as a person and I want to hug her and say thank you for not judging me and my clear plastic prison issued bag and worn out sneakers.

"I used to be a medium." I run my hand over the t-shirt stretched thin across my chest. "I've, ah, grown, so it's probably bigger?"

With a nod, she walks into the tiny shop to rummage through the clothing racks and I turn my attention to the mini fridge. I don't even open it, instead I reach for the bowl of fruit on top and choose a ripe red apple. It's so crisp and juicy. It's fresh and perfect.

Not from a mass bag of apples like the prison would have. All bruised and banged up, just like the inmates. The apples nobody else wanted.

It's such a simple pleasure to have the juice of an apple squirt and spill out. I catch myself laughing as I wipe my chin and the kind woman smiles at me.

"Sorry, it's been a while since I've had an apple like that. I must look ridiculous."

"Simple pleasures are some of the best things in life. Don't be sorry. It makes my day to make people happy." She flops a pile of clothing on a chair in a change room. "Finish your apple and try those on."

For the first time in years, I feel a small lift that it'll be okay, and I pull the curtain closed. There's no way I can afford all the clothes she laid out, nor do I have a place for them. But I try them all on simply because it's good to feel anything other than the harshness of prison issued garments against my skin. Most of them fit too, she chose well.

I pick three pairs of jeans and four t-shirts. I can buy socks and underpants at Walmart for cheap and shoes too if there's nothing here. But when I exit the change room with my choices, she's actually laid out a few pairs of shoes that might fit.

Trying them all on, I settle on the black pair that feel like a dream since they're almost new and still have cushion to them. Not like mine that are so worn they may as well be flaps of plastic strapped to my feet.

"I think you said you needed a backpack. This one might not be the best print, but I think it's the best quality for what you need."

She shows me a cheetah print pack and I laugh. An honest laugh, but it dies quickly when I remember what I need it for.

"Uh, so how much do I owe you?"

I fumble out my envelope of money and wish I had been brave enough to take my wallet out of the clear bag when I was in the van.

Her hand is quick to cover mine.

"It's a 'pay what you can' store. If you can pay anything right now, feel free. But if you can't, you leave here with your head held high and come back when you can."

She folds the clothes and starts packing them into the backpack for me. "You're very kind. Thank you."

"Don't thank me, love. I'm just here to remind people we're all in this together and kind is the best way to be. I know you think people will think you're a bad person because you have tattoos and it's hard to hide you just left the detention center. But I'm not one of those people."

At least she didn't call it a facility.

"And why not? Why are you helping me like this?"

Sliding my full pack over to me, she smiles again. "Because I can and I want to." She scrawls a name and number on a card and passes it to me. "This is a friend of mine who might be able to offer you a job when you're ready. Call him and tell him Molly sent you. He'll get you back on your feet."

Taking the card, I slide it into the envelope with the money and back into my pocket.

"Thank you, Molly. I don't know if I'll ever repay you. But I'm going to try."

"Just take care of yourself... " Her words hang and I realize she's waiting for a name.

I thrust my hand forward. "Dante."

"Take care of yourself, Dante."

Leaving the store, I'm thankful for the spring jacket Molly also picked for me since the rain is lightly falling. Flipping up the hood, I carry my backpack with the next mission of finding a place to sleep for the night.

I checked out of the night shelter as soon as I could this morning. I accepted their bag of toiletries with gratitude, as well as the hot shower. With my newish clean clothes I hope I can pass inspection at the bank.

My wallet still has my bank card and the account number I used to have. I haven't used it for three years, but if I can prove I'm me, I should be able to access my bank account. If I can access the money I set aside before my life fell apart, I'll have a little more breathing room. My short term plan depends on this money. It's not a great plan, but I have to start somewhere.

When I reach the counter, the teller asks me to insert my card and when it asks for my pin number I enter the four digit code I'll never, ever forget and hold my breath. The machine beeps to remove my card and my shoulders droop. First obstacle successfully down.

"Dante, there's a message for me to update your contact info. The account has been dormant for a long time. Was there a reason for that?"

My mouth goes dry as her friendly eyes wait for my response. "Ah... "

The lady at the teller next to me clutches her purse tighter, and it feels like every set of eyes in the place are burning holes through me. I force myself to swallow and lean closer.

"Can I speak with someone privately?" I don't want anyone to hear my details. I'm tired of everyone knowing my business.

"I can take care of it here, it's not an issue."

She smiles back at me in full customer service mode.

I swallow the lump building in my throat. "I don't want anyone overhearing. Please." I plead, hoping she doesn't keep pushing me to spill everything here.

Her smile drops, but just a little.

"Give me a minute."

She hops off her chair and disappears to the back, and I'm acutely aware of the hidden camera in the corner. The fact I'm carrying a backpack probably doesn't help either. I wipe at my brow with the back of my hand.

"You can come with me, Dante." The teller holds open a half door for me and I follow her through.

She leads me to an office with the word manager on the door in a very official and gilded plate. In the office, I'm introduced to an older woman. Even with her hair in a stern bun, her smile sets me at ease. I bet she's someone's amazing mom and grandmother. "Mr. Perrish, I'm Mary." She gestures to the chair in front of her desk. "Please sit and let me help. Darla tells me you need to update your account and you want privacy."

I settle into the chair and place my bag between my feet. "Thank you, it's just... people judge you and I've only just come back here and... " I let my voice stop when I realize what I have to say. "She needs to update my info and... I'm homeless right now." My voice cracks and the woman doesn't even flinch. "I have identification proving I'm me and where I've been for the last three years. But I need the money in this account, please."

Never did I think I'd ever find myself in a situation like this. Begging for someone to let me access money that's mine while I admit I'm homeless. Talk about a bitter pill of life disappointment.

"I understand, and I'm sorry to hear that. We have customers without fixed addresses who hold bank accounts. We can straighten it out for you. But you'll need to show me your identification and I'm going to ask you some questions to make sure I've followed all the protocol before I can release any funds, okay?"

For the next thirty minutes I recite everything on my current file and stop short of revealing my cock size, which I should've because she has enough information on me to become me at this point.

But when she returns to the office and hands me a thick envelope, I could cry.

"This is a lot of money to carry around, Dante. Knowing where you might be sleeping and going around with this much money on you makes me nervous. Are you sure you want it all right now?"

"I'm sure. It's buying me a place to stay. I won't be holding on to it for long."

She passes me the envelope and I stuff it into my backpack, relieved I can get on with my plan.

"Thank you so much for helping me, Mary. When I get a job, I'm using this bank again."

She shakes my hand. "Good luck to you, Dante. I look forward to seeing you with that first paycheck." She walks me to the front lobby and I'm buoyed with my victory today.

Zipping my coat up outside, I hit the sidewalk again for my next step.

Chapter 2

Colby

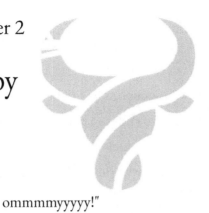

"**M**ommmmmyyyyy!"

The kid who was far too old to be throwing such a fit in public wailed at the top of his lungs. It sent my already throbbing migraine into the next level of pain.

"Jarvis, please just pick one. I said you could have one candy."

Of course, the kid has a douchey sounding name to go along with his preppy clothes and his PTA mom. Mom's pained smile finds my own and if the kid doesn't stop having a meltdown, I'll be having one of my own.

"Excuse me, Jarvis." My tone leaves no room for his shit and he immediately stops with the wailing. "The store closes in five minutes. If you don't choose, you'll get nothing."

The mom is both shocked at my abrupt tone and I'd like to say appreciative for getting the boy to listen. But you know how some parents can be. Today is not a good day to try my patience and good customer service packed its shit hours ago.

The boy immediately grabs a bag of sour caterpillars, hands them to his mother, and I quickly ring up the sale. As soon as they're out the door, I flip the sign to closed, turn the lock and head straight to my office. Stopping in the bathroom, I run a cloth under cold water before laying down on the loveseat and pulling a blanket over me.

Of all the days to get a migraine, it had to be today. The one day I wanted to do something fun and stop reliving my worst memory. Because as sure as the sun rises each day, I'm going to replay it in my mind. That stormy day, my world came to an abrupt end with a crash, and nothing has ever been the same.

Well, it sort of stayed the same on the outside, but on the inside, my heart died. Withered up like the plant I left too long without water in my apartment.

I miss him.

"Don't. Please don't go there right now, stupid brain. Just let me get over the pain in my head before you make my heart hurt again."

My voice fills the dark office, and I wince at how loud it sounds. When I'm sure the nausea has passed, I swallow the pills and pray for a decent sleep to escape from at least some of the pain.

In my darkened office, I fumble for the lamp and switch it on. It's just after midnight. I slept for seven hours! At least the headache is gone. Thank the gods for small miracles. Grabbing a granola bar from the shelf, I turn the store lights on to complete the cleanup I didn't do before I had to lie down from the migraine.

The main street of Bloomburg is bathed in the fluorescent glow of streetlights, and I smile at the hanging flower baskets the town has on each one of the antique street lights. It's so old school, charming and pretty. Three years ago, I moved back here when I purchased the business of the old-fashioned candy store. It was perfect and exactly what I dreamed of when I knew I wanted to be a business owner.

Well, I'd start with a candy shop and see what else it could become, but retro candy was always a passion of mine. As a child, I hunted it down. I ordered it online, and I saved packages. I was equally addicted to the product and the cool packages.

How could you not want to be surrounded by sugar and candy all day long? It's impossible to not stay in a good mood when your daily company is happy packages and the sweet smell of saccharine goodness.

I'm sure my parents didn't dream of me owning a candy shop called Lick it Up. Yes, I loved the song too, which is partially what made me name it that. But once upon a time, far too long ago, someone I loved once made a joke about naming a candy store Lick it Up and it just stuck with me, much like the gum I had stuck in my hair as a kid.

Unlike the gum, I didn't just cut it out and move on. Not me. I have to live with those memories every day and grind salt in my own wounds.

My phone pings with a text and it can only be one person checking on me this late.

Landon: Are you okay? I woke up and you weren't home yet.

Colby: I'm fine. Had a bitch of a migraine and just woke up. I'll be home once I'm done with the closing.

Landon: Do you need me to come and help?

Colby: I'm good.

Landon replies with a heart emoji, and I stuff the phone back in my pocket. My roommate cares. He more than cares, he loves me. As best friends do, nothing more. It's nice to have that one person who does care in some way, though. He's just not the one I want texting me at midnight checking on me.

"I'm such a fucking hopeless fool."

Shaking my head at my own unrealistic hopes and dreams, I lock up and drive myself home. The best thing about tomorrow is that it's Sunday. Sunday means it's my day with my best girl, my horse Babe. At least my migraine didn't get in the way of that.

My little red Honda Civic rolls through the arches for The Broken Horn Ranch and Landon vibrates in this seat.

"I still get to ride too, right?" he asks me for the sixth time in the last half hour.

"Lan, yes. Now stop."

I park the car close to the horse barns and turn to him.

"Dan is fine with it. You've done this before. You're fine. He loves the horses getting any kind of extra attention."

He nods like he's listening and I sigh because he's really not, but I love him. I couldn't have asked for a better best friend, but sometimes it's hard to pull him out of his own head and convince him people at the ranch are okay with him riding with me. He's the kindest person you'll ever meet, but he's always insecure about his size. He's a proverbial mountain of muscle and at six foot seven inches tall he's intimidating as hell. But he's just a giant teddy bear. One I've hugged and cried on many nights.

Together we enter the barn and I find Alec in there already almost done cleaning the stalls for the day.

"Alec! What're you doing? This is my job on Sundays."

The well muscled ranch hand leans on his pitch fork after shaking out new bedding in my horse's stall. He wipes the back of his hand across his forehead and a friendly smile fills his handsome face. If my heart wasn't glued to someone else, I'd probably have a crush on him. No, scratch that. I definitely would have a crush on him.

"I took one of the rescues out in the ring this morning and since I had nothing else on the agenda, I thought I'd give you a hand."

"But how do I earn Babe's keep when you keep doing the work for me?" I whine.

"You'll more than make up for the odd day I take care of the stalls for you. Don't even worry about it. Just say thank you, okay?" His smooth, deep voice is enough for me to stop my protest.

He spoils me and I know I should be grateful, but it doesn't always come easy for me.

"Thank you. I'll bring you one of those surprise bags next week you like so much."

Alec shakes his head and returns to his task with a grin on his face. I really need to accept he just loves to help when he can. I'm still going to bring him a surprise bag, though. Seeing a grown man excited over a paper bag of candy always makes me happy.

"Who do I get to ride today?" Landon follows me to the pasture with a halter and lead of his own.

"I think Lucy or Linus would be good. Lucy, preferably, for you." I smile his way before calling out to my horse, Babe. She lifts her head, and with a swish of her tail, she walks my way. She's a beautiful chestnut brown quarter horse and as much as I love her, she also reminds me of the man who broke my heart. Babe is mine, but she bonded to him too when he came to live with me and mom. Her name was our inside joke. We used to call each other that, the one summer we finally crossed the line from stepbrothers to something more. Two boys and a horse living a carefree summer full of sunbeams, hope, and stolen kisses. It was the best summer of my life.

I love Babe. Some days she can't help ease the ache, but she doesn't deserve to be cast aside like yesterday's garbage in the way that I was. Besides, she's the best horse and I love riding. Even old painful memories won't keep me away from that.

A thunder of footsteps starts our way with several of the ranch horses heading towards us. They've seen my carrot.

Landon laughs like a crazed hyena as the horses pull up short, sniffing over us and looking for more. He feeds his carrot to Lucy as he slips the halter over her head and Babe pushes her way through the crowd to reach me.

Her soft nose rubs on my cheek with a snicker and I slip the halter over her while she finds the carrot in my coat pocket.

"My beautiful girl," I croon. "Ready for a ride today? A new meadow, maybe?" My hand slides along her dark brown neck and she blinks her long lashes at me. God, I love this horse.

Landon and I lead the horses to the tack barn and saddle them. We pack up supplies in the saddlebags for lunch and anything else needed for a long trail ride. Dan owns at least one thousand acres of ranch and past the last fence is a gorgeous open meadow, perfect for quiet intimate moments or just a place to clear your head. Today I need option B.

An hour's ride will take us to the trailhead and another thirty minutes takes us to the meadow. During the ride time, Landon and I banter about my store, the ranch, his family, and our plans for the week. Neither of us brings up what day it is, but he knows.

He knows what's pushing me into the peaceful quiet of nature with my horse for so many hours. I do too and I loathe it, but it's the only way I can deal with it. Until another three hundred and sixty-five days pass and it's in my face again.

We ride in silence up the single file path on the last stretch until finally we enter the meadow. The lush green grass and wildflowers are just beginning to paint the landscape in the late spring. It's like seeing a watercolour painting come to life. The scent of honeysuckle lingers as the late morning sun warms the plants and air. A small stream bubbles at the edge of the clearing and it's here we dismount so the horses can drink and graze.

"Every time you take me here I'm in awe at how beautiful it is."

Landon spreads a blanket out for us and flops down.

"One day, I'd like to get brave enough to camp out here. One of those tiny tents with the skylight so I can watch the stars without being chewed alive by mosquitoes."

Landon squeezes my hand in support. I say the same damn thing every time I bring him here.

"And you'll spend it with someone special. You'll talk for hours and sleep naked in a too small sleeping bag," he adds with a chuckle.

The sadness rolls over me as I remember that last conversation with the only person I've ever given my heart to. He still has it, and I'm convinced it's why I'm so empty. Squeezing my eyes closed, I relive that day. How we made promises to each other, and we were going to leave together no matter what our parents had to say.

Love had no obstacles. We were lost in our happiness that day. Giddy with the possibilities that were just around the corner. We'd be high school graduates and the college was picked out. We had our housing lined up together. Nothing was going to get in our way. But he obviously kept something from me. Why did he leave that night and not come back?

I loved him, and he loved me. Or so I thought.

The rough pad of Landon's thumb brushes across my cheek to chase the tears that snuck out.

"Let it out, Colby. It's why we come here."

Babe whinnies softly when I glance her way. She was there. Maybe she remembers it too.

"I wish I could just let it go, Landon. I really do. I've dated. I've tried to have boyfriends. I can't get past him."

"The heart is hard to convince sometimes and overrides what our brain says. He was special to you. There's no shame in that."

"We were special to each other. He didn't lie to me about his feelings. I know he couldn't have, but he just left me. No note, no call. He fucking vanished, and I'd hate him for that if I could just stop being so stupid in love with him to do it." My voice hitches as the familiar ache takes hold.

Landon's hand squeezes tighter and I curl into him. Welcoming his strong arms of comfort until his stomach growls, and I take the hint to unpack our snacks.

"Did you make those little triangle sandwiches I like?"

Setting the containers on the blanket between us, I pop the lid, and he grins.

"It's just cucumbers on bread, you know. You can make these anytime you want."

"I know, but they taste better when you do it and you cut them up cute for me." He winks and takes the container offered with his sandwiches. The band around my chest loosens just a little.

"Have you ever been in love, Lan? Love so hard you can't breathe sometimes?"

He cocks his head. "Once. But I think it was because she was wearing too much perfume." He snorts, and I punch him playfully.

"Do you ever want to be in love?" I ask.

He finishes his sandwich and reaches for another. "I dunno. If it makes me feel like you do every May thirty-first, I'm not sure I want to."

"It was great before he left. If you knew me when it was all sunshine and rainbows I wasn't like this. I smiled more and I felt like I could take on the world. Nothing could stop me because I was in love. I'm not normal, okay?" I laugh, truly because I know there're people who break up and move on with their lives just fine. Or people who aren't in love and are perfectly happy. But I'm firmly stuck on the one who left me without a trace.

Landon turns to me, eyes serious.

"Most people don't have the extra hurdle of falling in love with their stepbrother, Colby. Cut yourself some slack, okay? It's hard."

He leaves to go retrieve the horses who have wandered farther away and I pluck a dandelion from the ground next to me.

Landon has a point. I should cut myself some slack, but why is it so hard?

Chapter 3

Dante

A final pass of the truck stop shower room confirms I'm not leaving anything important behind, and I let the door close behind me. Last night, I parked my car amongst all the rigs with the hope it was safer there than a random parking lot for sleeping.

Most of the transports had sleeper cabs and the truck stop was also a spot to have a hot meal and shower before hitting the road early the next day. I figured it would be a good place for me for the same reasons and add a sliver of safety. I purchased a car at a used car lot right after I drained my bank account. Paying cash knocked the price down and it was no luxury car. But a few thousand dollars only goes so far and I know I can't depend on the useless bus pass the prison gave me to get around. It's not only a means of transportation, it's also my new home.

I'm now the proud owner of a 1987 silver Chevy Chevette. It has no power windows or locks. No fancy electronic features either. But it has power steering, minimal rust and still runs well. The back seat will do for stretching out if I don't want to recline and sleep in the front seats. It's not much of a stretch out, but it's an option.

The hatchback locks with a secure cover to hide my few belongings as well.

With the help of my probation officer this week, I have a temporary address. It's a postal box for now, but it provides enough for ownership details and license plates. Insurance is a problem I'll have to deal with another day. Thankfully, the woman was compassionate as to why I couldn't provide the information yet.

Although I was warned to not get caught without it. But I have a roof over my head for now and, most importantly, transportation to a job. Without a job, I won't be able to keep eating and find a place to rent. I don't want to live in a car forever, even if it's cheaper than an apartment. Nor do I want to be by myself.

Last night I finally built up the courage to dig the photo out of my wallet. It was cracked and worn, but it was there and I smiled when I saw his face pressed against mine, while my heart shattered all over again. I don't know if he'll even want to see my face again. But I hope so.

Please let him still love me. I need to explain.

I placed the photo carefully back in the wallet with only some of my remaining money. I hid the rest under a loose seat cushion in the back seat. After packing away all the evidence of sleeping in my car in the hatchback, I drive carefully to the employment office with the card Molly gave me.

It simply says, *Dan – Broken Horn*. I hope it's something animal related, but I'll take anything right now. There's not many people who are willing to work with those who have criminal records. I'll have to deal with that mistake for the rest of my life, but it's worth it if my dad kept up his end of the deal. Colby is my priority and always will be.

The employment office is quiet when I arrive and I sign in with a counselor. She gives me a passcode to a computer terminal and an instruction sheet for logging in to various job boards. Next to the computer there's a phone, and without pulling up job boards or building a resume, I call Dan first while my courage is high. He answers on the first ring.

"Hello, Dan speaking."

My throat closes up at the sound of the cheerful voice and I stamp down the surge of hope.

"Uh, hi Dan. My name's Dante. Um, Molly gave me your name and said to give you a call. For work. I'm... ah, I need a job."

Not my smoothest pitch. But the nerves have me in a chokehold.

"Hi Dante! Thanks for calling. I'd love to help you out. This is perfect timing, actually. Do you have any means of transportation or know the area well?"

With Dan's kind tone, my hope soars from my feet to the ceiling.

"I used to know it well. It's been awhile. I just moved back, but I can get to you."

The smile in his voice reaches me through the phone.

"Great! If you have a pen, I'll give you some directions and if you're free to come out right away, I'll see what I can find for you. I need labour right now. Does that work?"

I want to shout for joy and dance until I'm out of breath.

"Yes! I mean, I'd love that. I have a pen."

Dan rattles off the names of side roads and landmarks and how to find The Broken Horn Ranch, with a promise of explaining what it's about when I get there. When I hang up the phone, I could float out of the office.

"I have an interview!" I blurt to the lady at the reception and she whoops with joy, offering her hand for a high five.

"Good luck!"

Tripping over my feet, I can't get to my car fast enough. With the speed of an eighty-year-old driver, I follow the directions on the paper and eventually find myself driving under the arched metal sign of the Broken Horn Ranch. The main house stands out, a large log home, and I carefully park in front of the sprawling farmhouse.

"Okay, this is it. Please let him like me."

The car door protests and I step out, carefully pushing the lock button out of habit, and I climb the porch steps. Before I can knock, the door swings open and it can only be Dan greeting me. A swirling mop of unruly brown hair and a smile that could outshine a thousand suns greets me.

"You must be Dante!"

He stretches a giant mitt of a hand towards me and I straighten my shoulders to return the handshake.

"Nice to meet you, sir."

His booming laugh fills the air. "Please, just Dan. There are no sirs in this place." He sweeps his arm behind him. "Come in, let's talk."

Moo!

A little pink nose pops over the side of a pen. There's a cow, well, a calf in his living room.

"Uh, you keep cows inside usually?"

"No, not usually. She's an exception. This is Ash. Come say hi."

He flags me over with the enthusiasm of a four-year-old. When he reaches over the pen to pet the little calf's ears, I notice the large patch of missing fur and puckered skin.

"Aw, poor thing. What happened?"

His face softens as a giant slab of wet cow tongue swats at my arm and I chuckle. She's a cute one.

"I rescued her from a barn fire. Her sister, Ember, is out in the barn. Ash, though, her wounds were concerning me with all the spring bugs. I didn't want her to get infected. So I brought her inside for a few days until it heals up well enough then I'll bring her back to her sister." Another playful scratch behind the ears and Dan motions for me to sit at the dining room table, much to the displeasure of the calf who moos in protest at being left alone.

"Can I get you anything to drink? Coffee or something?"

"No si- I mean, no thank you, Dan."

Relaxing back into the chair, his eyes while kind, study me. Not judging, more like assessing me and what brought me here.

"Tell me how you've been around animals. You didn't even bat an eye to see there was a calf in my house and you even approached her without nerves. You've been around cows before?"

"Not cows, but horses. Dogs, cats and lots of smaller ones. Horses are the only large animal I'm familiar with."

Visions of lazy summer days, a favourite horse and stolen kisses in the hayloft dance through my mind, but I shake them clear.

"I, uh, had a horse as a teenager. She was great. I love all animals, really."

Dan leans forward, arms on the table as he studies me.

"Broken Horn Ranch is a lot of things, but its main purpose is a rescue. I started rescuing large animals whenever I could, because they tend to be viewed as just animals and nothing else." He nods towards Ash. "That calf was going to be euthanized just because she was a cow. Her wounds aren't critical, but she needs care. I have a pot belly pig who got too big for the owner's house, horses who couldn't be saddled, sheep born with facial deformities, and the list goes on. People call me when they think I can rescue them."

"Wow. That's so fucking fantastic." My eyes bulge when I realize I've sworn in front of a potential employer and my cheeks burn. "I'm so sorry. I shouldn't have said that."

His giant grin returns. "If you can't drop an f-bomb here, Dante, you might stand out like a sore thumb."

Dan walks to the kitchen and returns with two glasses of water, setting one in front of me.

"I'm a helper, Dante. Animals are just part of the big picture. But before I agree to help you, I need to know your story. I need to know you can fit in here and there's no risk to my staff or my boyfriend." He takes a drink before leaning back again. "Before you start, that's the first thing you need to be okay with. I'm gay, it's not a secret and my boyfriend is here often. If that doesn't sit well with you, we can part ways now because I have no tolerance for disrespect of any kind."

. I swallow hard and stare into his eyes. "No problem at all, Dan. I'm ah, very accepting. I've got your back on that one."

He nods, understanding what I don't directly say with a subtle nod. "Good. Then carry on. And nothing you say to me leaves this room, okay? I don't share it with my partner or other staff or anyone else. Even Molly."

"How do you know Molly?" I ask.

"We were very close friends in high school." A fond smile sits as he speaks. "My first love, you could say. She's a wonderful woman."

"She is. I'm not sure how I was lucky enough to run into her that day, but she really made a difference for me. One day I'm going to pay her back."

He chuckles. "You go ahead and try. She'll probably buy you something else you need with it or just drop it into a donation jar. But I understand why you want to."

Taking a sip of water, I gather my thoughts to figure out what or how to explain to Dan what brought me to where I am now. Do I give him the full version or keep it strictly to the reason I was in prison?

"When I was nineteen, I was forced to make a choice. Leave home without a word, or have someone I cared about hurt in a way I couldn't bear to have happen. I left and I was on the street." Wiping my hands on my pants, I swallow thickly as the memory of that day burns in my chest. I wasn't actually on the streets since my father had it all planned, but I'll leave that part out for now.

"I was approached with an easy way to make money. I was a drug runner. I delivered drugs from the manufacturer to the dealer on the street. In return, I had a nice place to stay and the cupboards always had food."

With a shaking hand, I take a bigger gulp of water.

"I got caught one night. Thankfully, with not enough drugs on me to do a longer sentence, but I was caught. Because I didn't give out any names of suppliers, I was given the max they could for my offense. I spent all three years at Montrose Penitentiary. I never did the drugs myself, just so you know. I barely even drank. Clean as a church mouse. I just... "

Those years locked away with no contact from anyone almost killed my spirit. But seeing the light in the blue eyes of the boy I still loved was what kept me going. Knowing he was out there living his best life made the sacrifice seem worth it.

"Do you have any family, Dante?" Dan asks gently.

I shake my head. "They're still alive, but... I don't belong with them anymore."

His hand reaches over and takes mine in a squeeze. Part of the deal to keep Colby safe was to never contact my dad again. I'm supposed to stay away from Colby too, but it's time to change that.

"I've only been out for ten days. I don't want to be homeless forever, and one day...there's a person I want to find. To see him again and tell him I'm sorry. Maybe see if... see if he might still think about me."

"Do you need a place to stay, too? Or just a job?"

"I can bounce around the shelters and I've got my car for now, too. I need a job. I didn't graduate high school or go to college. I missed all that. My resume is shit except for the farm experience I had when I was a kid."

Dan grins. "Well, I just happen to have a farm. Tell me what you can do."

"I can do anything. The crappiest jobs. I can fix small motors a little and I'm really good with horses. I'm strong. I can do manual labour. Whatever you need, I can do." My voice cracks. "I'm not above any task, Dan. I won't make you regret it."

"Dante, you're hired. I actually do need help with some things, too. So it's not pure charity. We need to get some fields seeded and lots of other work, too. I'll pay you under the table for now until you can get an established address and such. That's not a problem for me, so don't worry about it. Six hundred dollars a week for ten hour days. That's close to minimum wage with no deductions. If you're happy with that, make it through the summer and want to stay, we'll look at getting you on the payroll after. You'd make less because you'll be paying taxes and reporting income, of course, but it's proof you're employable." He lets me digest his offer and takes our glasses to the sink.

I must have done something good in my short life to keep crossing paths with kind people. I don't know how to ever repay the kindness, but I know one day I will.

"I'd really like to work for you. You have no idea how much I appreciate this si- Dan."

He smiles at me as he walks me out. "I'm pretty sure I do, Dante. Can you be here tomorrow morning at 8 A.M.?"

"Fuck, yes!"

His booming laugh makes me smile harder.

"That's what I like to hear!"

Feeling more alive than I have in the last five years. I drive back into town with a renewed hope I'll one day get my second chance at the life I was denied.

Chapter 4

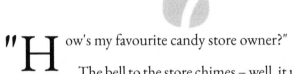

Colby

"How's my favourite candy store owner?"

The bell to the store chimes – well, it plays a line from the famous song associated with my store Lick it Up – and I stop rearranging a lollipop display. Landon has arrived in full Landon glory. A mountain of best friend muscle and sunshine, fresh from the gym and carrying a take out tray with what I already know is my favourite coffee.

"I'm only your favourite because you get free candy."

He plucks the coffee from the tray and hands it to me. The salted caramel aroma greets me as I take a sip.

"Fuck this is good. Thanks, Lan."

He plops a bag on the counter, "They had those blondies you like today, too. You can save it for later."

Sipping from the straw of his own more healthy smoothie, he tosses the take out tray and perches on the stool behind the cash register.

"Are you buttering me up? Coffee and a blondie on the same day. You either love me or want something," I joke.

Landon sighs, "Colby, you were up all night crying. Which I know because you asked to sleep with me, remember? I'm checking in on my friend who I love to make sure he's okay, so cut the crap."

I should've known he'd not let it drop. I probably shouldn't have used him as a human tissue last night either. But it was a rough night and I needed comfort.

Walking over, I wrap my arms around him and squeeze.

"I'm sorry. That was an asshole thing to say. I'm okay. I just let it all build up and last night was... "

"You letting go, maybe?" His big hand rubs my back in his gentle way, "Are you finally moving on, Colby? Cuz I felt you were different last night."

"I thought about what you said and being easier on myself. It's not healthy and I shouldn't keep carrying a torch for someone who's gone and never coming back." Pacing to the front of the store I stare out the picture window covered in fun pics of kids in a bubble gum blowing contest. Last night was me letting go in a way. I can't go back to that time and Dante isn't in my life.

I turn back to face Landon. "I'm twenty-four years old with my whole life ahead of me. I need to get out there, so you're right. Last night *was* different. I decided to start letting go and it hurt."

"If it counts for anything, I think you're doing the right thing. If you need me you know I'm always there. Even if you change your mind later. Whatever it is, Colby, I've got your back."

Why can't this be the guy I'm in love with? Aside from the fact he's straight, he'd be a perfect partner.

"I know you do and I love you for putting up with my mood swings and migraines and all the other crazy shit I put you through."

He shrugs with a grin. "Well, I mean, you sell candy. And you let me have it when I want. That's a dream relationship for me. I'm not going anywhere." I laugh as he picks a bag of gummy fish from a display. "Can I take these with me?"

"Of course, but for the love of god, floss after. Those things aren't good for your teeth."

He flashes his pearly white grin, "I'm good, my man. Before I go, do you need my help with anything here? Any heavy boxes for lifting or anything?" He flexes his biceps with a laugh and I shake my head.

"I'm covered for today, but I'll call if it changes."

With an exaggerated wave he leaves and I'm left by myself for a short while before the afternoon traffic picks up. The kids finished with school for the day all trail through one after another spending their allowance and no doubt keeping the dentists busy. But the sales and the distraction are welcomed.

Tonight there's no migraine to have me crash in my back office. There's just a heaviness that comes when you accept the person you've been waiting for to return your whole life isn't coming.

Before I lock up for the night I drift to the front store window and stare at the image of a tiny pink stick, a Fun Dip Lik-a-Stix to be more accurate. It's there hidden in the corner and not totally out of place in a candy store window. I should take it down and throw it out, since it's only there for one person and he'll never see it anyway.

I can't deal with it now, though. Not yet. Baby steps will have to get me through this.

Instead I set the alarm behind me and drive home.

I've made it through the week with no more breakdowns. Yay, me!

No more crawling in with Landon and crying and I feel like I've finally turned a corner. A huge corner that goes on for days – kind of like when you drive through Saskatchewan – but still, progress is progress. But an email from my mom and stepdad saying they want to come and see me soon has my forward progress lurch to a halt. I love my mom and miss her, but her husband not so much. I tolerate him because he loves my mother but we've never gotten along. He came into my mom's life after my dad had been gone for a few years. Even at the tender age of fourteen, I knew she needed help.

When Brian showed up, and kept showing up, I had to accept I'd be sharing mom with someone else. When he brought a teenage son of his own, it made it worse. Well, until I went and fell in love with him, that is. Then Brian was an alright guy for making us both smile again.

But once Dante disappeared, my dislike of Brian intensified. I blamed him for not finding Dante or knowing what happened to him. I blamed him for anything that made me sad and I was unfair, I know that. I still didn't like him, though. And if he hadn't stepped in, mom might have had to sell Babe all those years ago. So, I tolerated him.

I respond to the email with a quick let me check my work schedule and I'll let you know and some other kind of nonsense to put it off. I'll deal with it later. Today is Sunday and I spend it with my horse, Babe. Every Sunday is Babe day no matter what, and if I don't get there early Alec might already have mucked the barn stalls.

Again.

I really don't want him to keep doing that.

Peeking into Landon's room, he's snoring soundly and I don't want to wake him. He's been working a lot of late nights at the gym. If he's not working, he's been studying. I know he loves being with the animals, but I'll go by myself today. He needs his rest.

The front door closes quietly behind me and I slip out to my car with my travel coffee mug. It's a twenty minute drive to the ranch and early mornings are the most beautiful time of day. I do some of my best thinking watching the sun rise. The email from my mom is stuck in my head even though I said I'd deal with it later.

I haven't seen mom since Christmas and Brian sometime before that. She came to Bloomburg for two days and stayed with me and Landon and it was great. I missed her, but something was off then. She very rarely traveled without him, but whenever I tried to bring it up she changed the subject. I knew better than to keep pressing her, so I chose to live in the moment and spend time with mom.

She even asked to visit the ranch to see Babe, and Dan had a sleigh ride running that day. We fed Babe treats and enjoyed the day with sleigh bells and hot chocolate before returning to town when she spoiled Landon and I with dinner. Before she left and I dropped her at the airport she brought up Dante, though. It was the first time she'd spoken about him in years and she hadn't been aware of us being in love. Or if she was, she never let me know or confronted me.

I had simply brushed her words aside, but now with my decision to move forward and the email of her and Brian wanting to visit has me remembering the conversation and I'm wondering if she was trying to tell me something.

"When Dante disappeared, it threw us all for a loop, honey. Matters of the heart are sometimes fueled by things we don't understand. By forgiving we can heal and move on."

Maybe she could tell I was still missing him. I didn't want to talk about it then, though, and her flight was called anyway. But in our conversations since, she's never brought it up.

Once I arrive at Broken Horn, I shove that memory aside and notice Babe is already in pasture which means Alec started early again despite my request not to.

When I enter the barn, Alec is indeed already working and I stomp my foot. A habit I haven't lost since I was an over dramatic eight year old.

"Alec! I asked you not to do this."

He pokes his head out of a stall and I instantly regret saying something.

"Hi, Colby. It's not what you think." He pinches the bridge of his nose and the lines under his eyes are so dark I'd swear he put the stuff athletes use for sun blocking on. "The old mare with one eye? Sally? She had colic really bad the last few days and... "

My heart plummets.

"Aw fuck, Alec. I'm so sorry. Are you okay?"

Alec has been part of the ranch since before I arrived, and he was attached to Sally. She was so timid at first and he worked so hard to befriend her. He was the only one she really trusted. Now she was gone and it obviously wrecked him.

"It's part of life, right? I'm sad, but I'll be okay. We had to put her down a few hours ago and uh, Dan has a place for them... when they die."

He swallows thickly and I know how broken he is to lose Sally. I'd be a mess if it was Babe.

I cross the space between us and throw my arms around him, hugging him with all the strength in my body. "I know. She loved you and you did what you could. Let me take care of the barn like I'm supposed to. Please. You do what you need to. Take some time, Alec. She wasn't just a horse."

He says nothing, but doesn't release the hug for a few moments. "Thanks. I should probably get some sleep."

"Well, you do look like shit," I tease.

I smile when he laughs back, happy to have eased the grief just a tiny bit. "You're a good one, Colby."

"I know, and I brought you this." I pull out two crumpled blue and red paper bags from my pockets and his eyes light up.

"Perfect timing. Thank you. I'll let you know what toy I get." He winks and stuffs them in his pockets. On the way out of the barn he pauses.

"Oh, I should give you a heads up, Colby. Dan has a new guy on staff and he might be around today. He was working hard covering things for me while I was with Sally. So if you see someone new, it's him."

"Thanks, I'll help him out if he needs anything."

Once Alec leaves I busy myself with finishing the chores. When I reach Sally's stall I notice Alec has her halter still hanging with her name tag and the fragility of life slams home. It could have been my horse. I hurry to finish up so I can spend as much time with Babe as she'll allow.

As always, she comes to me when I wave and call for her and I can't wait to spoil her for the day. I'll give her a bath and braid her mane and tail, and all the treats she can safely have.

"Hey there beautiful girl." She snickers and roots for the carrots she knows are in my pocket and I stroke her silky mane. "Spa day? You and me?"

There's no need for a lead, she follows me to the tack barn and waits while I prepare warm soapy water for her bath. She likes the massage part best with the nubby brush so I choose that and start working her coat while I talk to her. It's silly, but I think she understands sometimes.

"When I first got you, you were such a scrawny thing. All knees and legs, but you were so cute. I wanted to bring you inside that first night and my mom compromised. She let me sleep in a tent by the barn that night instead. I never begged my mom to buy me something like I did you. Did I ever tell you that?" Babe swishes her tail with a neigh and turns to look at me. "I won those riding lessons when I was a kid and fell in love with horses. The guy at the riding facility just happened to have a horse pregnant and we were first in line for you. As soon as I saw you, I knew you were the horse for me."

Babe reaches back to nuzzle my pockets for more treats and finds more carrots in my jacket. She butts her head against me as she chomps away and I pause to kiss her forehead.

"A guy at the boarding place helped saddle break you for me. Even he said you were a delight to train, did you know that?"

I pause to kiss her forehead again and scratch her ears. This horse got me through a lot and she'll get me through more.

"Remember the first summer I brought someone to meet you? He had these big brown eyes I could get lost in, just like yours. And he had these dark extra long eyelashes that were so beautiful, just like yours." I laugh softly. "He really liked you and sometimes he'd joke and call himself Babe so I'd give him more attention than you." My hand shakes as I hang up the towel after drying her and I start brushing her out.

"One day I did give him attention. Remember? You were there."

It was the best day of my life when I finally took the huge step of making an advance on my stepbrother. We were eighteen and just learning our way. I knew I liked boys, but I was still unsure about how to approach them and I was confident he felt the same as me. We were friends by then, close friends, and I knew I wanted him more than life itself. He was tall with broad shoulders and deliciously dark hair that never seemed to behave on his head. His deep soulful brown eyes were my Achilles heel. I always felt like his eyes told me everything his mouth didn't say. Both of us were dancing around what was brewing between us. But one kiss was all it took and I was gone.

I fell even harder for him after that kiss. Once we allowed ourselves to be with each other, it was like constantly floating on a cloud of the sweetest cotton candy while wrapped in the fuzziest blanket. It was safe, happy and I was in love.

"That day in the barn when we kissed for the first time, Babe. It was the best day of my life." I laugh as she whinnies and her lips brush my arm, like she's trying to tell me she remembers the kiss. "But he left me, Babe, and I think it's time I move on too."

Five years of silence and carrying a torch is enough.

"It's time for me to stop hurting. I should forgive him and move on. I deserve to be happy."

A shadow fills the entrance to the barn and a voice I could never, ever forget sends goosebumps up my arms and my stomach flopping.

"You deserve everything and more, Colby."

Hesitant footsteps approach, and my heart threatens to burst out of my chest. I want to throw myself in his arms and kiss him until I can't breathe. I want to run my hands all over him to make sure he's real.

But I can't.

When I raise my eyes to confirm if the voice belongs to the boy who crushed me, my breath catches. He's still so gorgeous, and it's him. Even behind the tattoos that weren't there before.

It's Dante. My Dante.

My eyes fly everywhere and catalogue everything about him. His face, his clothes, even the way his left work boot is untied. He should fix that before he trips. My mouth moves but nothing comes out.

When his hand brushes my shoulder with a tentative touch, I jump back. The familiar heat and prickles merge with the bubbling emotions I've been sharing with Babe and I explode.

"You don't get to touch me! How... where... what the hell are you doing here!? And, and... I can't deal with this right now."

I gulp in air and frantically turn to Babe, kicking over the now cold soapy water in my haste to get away from the one person I've been aching to see again. How can he just show up here now after all this time? I'm not ready.

"Colby, I...."

"Shut. The. Fuck. Up. Dante! You can't... you can't just show up while I'm with my horse and just... " I don't even know what I want to say, but I'm in no state to talk rationally with him. I thought if I ever saw him again it would be a sweet reunion, but today I'm raw and cut open. And I'm angry. With shaking hands I place a stool next to Babe and throw a leg over her back and urge her to the open barn door.

Once I'm in the yard of the ranch I push Babe to hurry towards the open field that leads away from the farm house and barns. Once it's safe to do so I dig in my heels to have her carry me away as fast as she can.

What kind of cruel world has the love of my life show up unannounced after five years, just days after I've decided to move on?

Chapter 5

Dante

When I recognized the gorgeous brown horse earlier this week, my heart soared. It was comforting to see such a large part of my past and know Colby couldn't be far away. I whistled, our special sound, and she snapped her head up with twitching ears. If a horse could wear a look of shock, Babe did. She remembered me and trotted over, even nudged around looking for treats. Although I'm not sure if that part is because Colby still spoils her or she remembers I brought the apple from my lunch every day.

But I should never have listened in while he was speaking to Babe. I couldn't help it. I wanted nothing more than to see him again, and his voice froze me to the spot. It was deeper now, but it's still the same sweet sound that transports me back to a happier time and place. When we were still innocent and had our futures ahead of us. Before both of us were broken into so many pieces, I wonder how we'll ever be able to be whole again.

I knew he'd be mad once I broke the silence, but I didn't think he'd storm out on me. I expected yelling and probably tears, but this was... a lot. It's hard to digest what I'm feeling right now.

Bending down, I clean up the mess he left from grooming Babe with a heavy heart. I hope I haven't fucked it all up.

"Hey, Dante! I just saw Colby go flying out of the yard bareback on his horse. Did he say anything? That's not like him. He's always so careful."

My boss's voice fills the silence of the barn and I turn to face him. I should have told him once I figured out the horse was the same one I used to know. Maybe I should have told him there was history with me and one of his boarders, but I didn't. Now I've possibly put Colby in danger if the tone of Dan's voice is anything to go by.

Sighing, I look up to the dust filled rafters.

"He left because of me." My voice wavers and I clear my throat.

Dan frowns and I know he's struggling to pull something together in his mind before he speaks and quite possibly tells me to leave. I'm just a guy with a prison record he offered to help. He has no allegiance to me. But Colby is sunshine and light and everyone's friend. He spreads happiness everywhere he goes and he's more Dan's friend than I could ever be.

I won't interfere with Colby's enjoyment of Babe. I'll leave to give him space before Dan tells me to.

"It's okay, Dan. I'll go. You tried to help and I'm grateful, but I don't want to cause any trouble."

Dan takes my arm as I try to push past him.

"You're not going anywhere. Help me understand why he left like he did, Dante. Because that man never, ever puts himself at risk or his horse. This isn't just you saying you don't like his hair style today." Dan's eyes bore into mine and the longer he looks I know he sees things I don't want anyone else to ever know. "Do I need to send someone after him?"

"I hope not. I think... I think he's just in shock to see me."

His grip relaxes on my arm and he stares off in the direction Colby went.

"I'm going to look for him on the quad if he's not back in an hour. He's usually here all day on a Sunday, but he won't be gone all day like that and he doesn't even have water with him."

"Should I leave?" My voice breaks and I look away. I need this job but, hell, I can't cause Colby anymore pain either.

Dan's voice soothes the wound I've just ripped open. "Maybe just today. Let him cool off, okay? Come back tomorrow as usual."

I nod, fully agreeing with his decision and step towards my car. "Dante." I stop and look over my shoulder. "You're still welcome here. We'll work it out and I'll see you tomorrow."

"Thank you," I croak.

Not giving Dan a chance to hear me scream, I drive out of the ranch's yard and down the dusty road before I pull over and scream until my throat is raw. I don't cry, there's no sense wasting tears. I cried enough of them already anyway and it didn't help. I want to be the one chasing after him and making sure he's okay.

But what do I do with myself now? It's not like I have an apartment to go to or a family to share the day with. I couldn't even go hang out at Molly's second hand store if I wanted. I'm not going to drive aimlessly and waste gas, but I need to do something and the day is still early.

Once in town again, I stop at the grocery store and purchase a loaf of bread and a small jar of peanut butter along with a package of apple juice boxes. It's not fine dining, but it will get me through today and tomorrow, at least. Armed with my meager rations, I head to the recreation area in town.

Hiking trails around the lake in Bloomburg used to be a fave thing to do when me and Colby were teenagers. Colby was such a nature nut, always taking me to places he called stunning or peaceful. At first I followed him because I just wanted to spend time with him. It didn't take me long to figure out I wanted more than just a walk on a trail with Colby.

The rec area has been upgraded a lot since I was here last. Landscaping and signage have been added and it has the air of a tourist stop now and not just a place for locals to spend the day. If the trail to the lookout still exists it's how I'll spend the day and hopefully get my mind in order. Looking around the parking lot that's mostly empty, I settle on a spot not too far away from the porta potty set up. I could spend the night here if it's not too heavily policed. It'd be a nice change from the rumbling of the transports all night in the truck stop, too.

Quickly making two peanut butter sandwiches, I shove a few juice boxes in my pockets with one of the sandwiches and eat the other one as I follow the marked paths leading to the look out. The path is well worn and I'm happy people still hike up here. Many afternoons were spent here with Colby out of the prying eyes of our parents, and it was here I accepted what he had come to mean to me. After we finally shared a kiss in the barn, this is where we came to plan and profess all the things people in love did.

Finally entering the clearing, I'm relieved to be alone with the whispering grasses and muted bird songs high in the trees. I don't know how I'm going to feel after spending time here, but I know I need to be here. Stepping over the guardrail, I push back the branches and fight my way through the underbrush to a pocket of peace. It's exactly as it was all those years ago and the tightness in my chest releases some. A giant rock sits in the middle of the space with a few fir trees around it and a mossy ground underneath, it's just like it always was.

"It's like a time capsule in here." I mutter as I settle into a comfortable spot on the bed of moss.

The fluttering of a silver condom wrapper stuck in the bushes confirms people still come here, but for now it's mine alone. Once upon a time it was mine and Colby's. A place where we could touch and laugh and kiss freely. If I close my eyes, I can still hear one of our last conversations here.

"Are you always like this?" Colby *teased and tickled my ribs. I couldn't help but laugh.*

"Like what? A brooding asshole angry at his dad for not letting him take the car out tonight?"

He bumps a shoulder to mine and together we sit on the bed of moss in the clearing. We heard about this secret spot from some college kids visiting and wanted to see if it was the great hook up place everyone says it is.

"At least I got my mom's car, though, and we could still go out."

I smile into his eternally happy face. The one I finally accepted I loved. The one I'd do anything to keep seeing.

Lacing his fingers through mine I kiss the back of his hand. "You did, she's a good egg. Just like you."

Resting his head on my shoulder we sit quietly in this little pocket until Colby shifts and straddles my lap. His eyes burn with an intensity I've never seen before. "Dante, I respect your wishes for not wanting to say anything to our parents until we leave for college. But I don't like it. I think my mom would be okay with it. She loves you."

"My dad won't like it. It will only make things tense at home. Please don't think I'm ashamed of it, Colbs. I love you. I just don't want to rock the boat."

He rests his forehead against mine and my hands grip his hips. I do love him. More than I thought was possible. He's my light and my future and I'd do anything for him.

"I love you too, and we'll make it work, D. Even if we're both working crappy jobs to pay the bills. You make me happy and I can't let that go. I was unhappy for too long before I met you."

"Your horse makes you happy, I'm a side piece." My lips twist as I try not to laugh and I creep my fingers under his shirt to feel his warm skin against mine.

"You're my missing piece. The stick to my Fun Dip." He chuckles before finally pressing his lips to mine and I chuckle back. Leave it to Colby to constantly bring up the day I gave him the Lik-a-Stix from my Fun Dip when his package came without one. A small gesture to me, but he looked at me like I hung the moon and stars that day.

I'd give him every Lik-a-Stix in the world if he'd look at me like that all the time.

I'm still alone when I open my eyes, but the memories of that day are still here. They're so clear I can feel the weight of Colby on my lap and the taste of the fruit roll up he ate in the car on his lips.

"Can't say I'm surprised you went ahead and opened a candy store. You talked about it, but I wasn't sure if you'd stick with it. You sure love your sugar."

I went to the library this week and googled Colby. Something I hadn't allowed myself to do it at all while I was in prison. I was paranoid his name would be found or seen and something terrible might happen. It was bad enough I'd already hurt him by leaving, there was no way I'd risk adding to it. So I avoided news from home. I avoided trying to contact my dad. He made it clear I was to never reach out under any circumstance.

Although I'm fairly certain he knew what happened to me. Being a police officer, he had to be aware of where I was, and the fact he'd stayed away from me was more likely to preserve himself. He'd already proven it was his best interests over mine. Good ole dad was his own priority.

Colby's name came up in my search with a newspaper article about how he was the new owner of the retro candy store. He'd only been the owner for eighteen months now and had plans to expand to an ice cream bar and renamed it *Lick it Up*. Even now the new store name makes me smile. 70s rock music and retro candy, two of his favourite things in one name and place. I made a note of the address in my head and avoided that street, though. I wasn't ready to see it or him yet. But it turned out to not be an issue anyway since I found myself working at the same ranch where he boarded his horse.

"I've created a bigger mess now without even trying, and I'm not sure how to fix it."

If Colby really and truly wants nothing to do with me, there's nothing here for me. I came back here for him. Sure, it was the closest town and I had nowhere else to go, but he's what keeps me here.

I drain my juice box and stuff the empty one in my pocket.

"I can't give up. He has to know I didn't just walk out on him. He'll listen, he just needs time to adapt to me being back."

At least that's what I'm going to try to convince myself with.

Brushing through the trees and back to the trailhead, I hike back down to my car. With nothing else to do, I set up my blankets in the back seat, brush my teeth outside, and settle in for the evening.

It's still early, and sometimes I don't dream about Colby.

Sometimes sleep is the only thing that makes the heartache go away.

Chapter 6

Colby

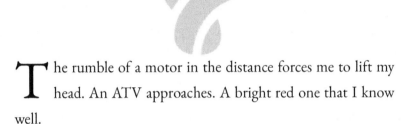

T he rumble of a motor in the distance forces me to lift my head. An ATV approaches. A bright red one that I know well.

"The cavalry has come, Babe."

I don't know how long I've been sitting on a stump at the edge of this far field. Nor do I know how far from the ranch I really am. I only know I stopped when I couldn't see it anymore. My thighs were burning with effort staying on top of a saddleless horse in full gallop and if I didn't stop when I did I may have taken a spectacular fall.

Of course, maybe that would have been better. I could have had something else to concentrate on instead of all these emotions I can't merge together.

The ATV comes to a stop and Babe continues grazing as Dan dismounts, walking my way with a bag on his shoulder.

He drops the bag on the ground next to me and shoves himself onto the stump until I'm forced to move over. I guess today is a no personal space kind of day.

"There's a perfectly fine and empty stump across from me, you know."

I glare at him, but he shrugs. "Meh, I don't like how it looks. Besides, I like to get close and snuggly."

He wiggles around on his side of the stump, bumping into me, and I shake my head. Leave it to Dan to make sure he lightens a moment.

"Before I ask you what the deal is, I want you to know I sent him home for the day. So you can come back and not face whatever it is that's going on with you two."

He passes me a bottle of water and without thanking him I pop the cap and draw a long swallow.

"There's nothing going on. Not anymore."

He hums under his breath and drinks from his own bottle. Before he arrived, the quiet of the trees was a comfort, but now the silence is just a stifling blanket on a too hot day. I don't owe Dan anything, but I actually do. He's been kind to me since I first showed up with my horse in a borrowed trailer when my mom announced her and Brian were moving off the country property and into the city. She and my stepdad weren't going to keep Babe. I rushed home from college to make sure she was taken care of. Me, a struggling student living in student housing with zero extra cash to care for a horse had to figure it all out and fast.

But Dan's reputation wasn't one built on rumours. He helped me unload her, gave her a stall and a place to store her tack. He introduced me to one of the ranch hands that day who would be caring for her, Alec. The only thing he asked was for me to come help around the ranch when I was able and Babe was still mine. I came whenever I had school break and helped with anything from fixing fences to mucking out stalls and tinkering with motors on the riding mowers and old tractors.

When I graduated and bought the store – thank goodness for angel investors – I had more financial security and I offered to pay. Dan refused and honoured our original agreement of simply helping when I could. Now I come every Sunday for chores and to ride Babe. In the summers I try to come on extra evenings depending on how busy work is. I bring bags of feed from town and leave them in the barns or bring over bulk bags of carrots for Alec to use with the horses. Dan won't accept payment, but if I brought gifts it was impolite to refuse. It was a loophole I took advantage of.

I don't need to give Dan an explanation about who Dante is or why I took off. But because all he's ever done is be kind to me and just give, I do owe him something.

"I haven't seen him for five years." My voice cracks from all the screaming I did earlier running away on the back of Babe. "We were – well, I was anyway – in love. Then he just disappeared and I've not heard from him since. I was a... fuck, it was like seeing a ghost and I panicked and ran."

A ghost of my past, one I finally decided I was ready to let go of. But now? I don't know what I want.

"You didn't let him explain why he was here or ask him anything?"

"Nope. Nothing." A dark laugh escapes. "Dan, the anniversary of the day he disappeared just passed. I decided it was long enough, and I was moving forward. For five years, I've carried a torch and had no idea what happened or where he was. Hell, I wasn't even sure he was alive. For him to just show up here, now... it's thrown me. I'm sorry for making you come after me and worry."

The silence descends again and I check on Babe, still close by, but I should take her back and finish what I started with her. And I don't know what else to tell Dan.

"I know it's not my place to pry, but even his family didn't have anything to tell you? Where he went? Anything?"

Biting my lip I stifle the sob that wants to escape me. Dan has no idea that's a sore spot.

"That's what makes it even worse, Dan. He's my stepbrother. I am his family." Standing up, I finish off the water bottle and hand it back to Dan whose face gives nothing away. "He didn't just leave me, but all of us. So excuse me for being angry about it."

His dad refused to address that his son was missing. With me moving away for college he immediately had my mom uproot and move to the city for a promotion. My mom loved Dante too, she was upset he was gone, but agreed leaving it all behind would be best. They didn't bother to ask me what I thought, though. I was already away at college. Other than relocating Babe, I had nothing but my memories of Dante.

Walking towards Babe, I speak over my shoulder. "Thank you for coming to check on me. I'll ride her back now and clean up, I'm okay."

Babe's a big horse. It's been a long time since I've tried to mount her bareback without something to stand on.

"Sorry girl, but I'm taking a running leap and it might hurt."

Babe is the best horse I've ever known and this is one of the reasons why. She stands still while I take two steps and launch myself onto her back and wiggle and pull myself up. Not once does she protest, but instead snickers and turns her head back to give me a look that says, "you're lucky I'm so good to you."

Panting from the effort, I take a moment to rest before asking her to take us home. The rumble from Dan's ATV sounds and I wave him off as the dust kicks up behind him.

When I came here this morning, I was ready to move a huge step forward and now I feel like I took a giant step back.

And my heart still doesn't know what to do.

The aroma of heavenly garlic greets me when I return home, and my stomach rumbles.

"Hey, I'm home!"

Landon pokes his head out of the kitchen with a scowl.

"You didn't wake me this morning."

"You needed your rest, and I needed some time to think, but turns out I should've brought you anyway."

"I can sleep anytime. I missed Babe and whoever my steed of the day was." He opens the oven door and removes a pan of lasagna. "But all is well because I made lasagna today and it smells pretty amazing if I do say so myself."

No, not all is well, Landon!

Landon chatters away, but I tune it out. Pulling out a chair in the kitchen, I flop down and lay my head on the table. The dull throb of a migraine kicked in on my way home. I know I should take the pills and just go to sleep, but my brain says otherwise. Landon's chatter stops and he places a glass of water in front of me.

"On a scale of one to ten where you at? Regular or prescription strength?"

Irrational anger fills me and I lash out at my best friend. "Maybe I don't want pills today, Lan! Maybe I'd like to just be and suffer more. I'm glad you cooked and had a great day but stop trying to.. to... to take care of me! I don't need any more people being in my face with their poor Colby looks."

And I can't take those words back. My best friend recoils as if I'd slapped him, and this day just keeps getting worse.

"Okay."

His single clipped word is enough and he goes back to slicing lasagna without another word. The first tear comes sliding down my cheek and I take my water glass to my room without another word. Once inside, I let the tears silently course down my cheeks while I find my meds. I'll make one good decision today and take the prescription meds before the throbbing in my head reaches vomit inducing pain.

"Colby?" A light knock on my door from Landon. "I'm sorry."

Opening the door, my mountain of a best friend looks as small as a garden mouse.

He brushes away the wetness on my cheeks. "Don't shut me out, ever. What's wrong? You never snap like that."

"I'm sorry, Lan." I run a hand through my hair with a sigh. "It's been such a fucking day and... fuck. He's here, Lan." There's no other way to tell him what's wrong. "Dante is here."

His kind eyes flash with a fire that scares even me. "Are you sure? What happened?"

With a heavy sigh, I invite Landon into my room. Landon waits as I shed my clothes from the day and pull on a pair of fuzzy pj bottoms. Flipping back my covers, I crawl into bed and Landon curls up behind me.

"Did you take the good pills, Colbs?"

His voice is a whisper in the dim room and the comfort of his hand on my back brings me back to the present.

"I did. Lan?"

"Hmm?"

"I'm sorry I was mean. It's been a long day. My head hurts and my heart hurts and I... I just don't know what I'm supposed to do."

"It's okay. I know you'd never be mean to me unless something was bothering you, which it obviously is. Take care of yourself for now and we'll deal with the rest later." He pauses, "You're sure it's him?"

Closing my eyes, his face is there for me to see. Every single part of him, only aged by five years, is burned into the back of my eyelids.

"Very sure. He was at the ranch. Babe even recognized him."

"You didn't know he'd be there? How is that possible?"

"I didn't even know he was in town, Lan. Five years away without a word and he shows up while I'm with Babe. I don't even know how I'm supposed to feel."

The heaviness of sleep starts to creep in at the edges and it's a chore to blink.

"You feel whatever you want to, Colby."

I drift off, grateful the pain in my head is at least taken care of for now and wonder how to deal with my heart.

Chapter 7

Dante

"Ouch! Son of a —"

Blood runs from my finger and I stick it in my mouth. Why I don't know, but I've always tried to make my cuts stop bleeding by sucking on them. Maybe I'm part vampire. Would a vampire bleed if they're dead, even?

"You should be wearing gloves, Dante." I shake away my vampire thoughts at his take no shit tone. "That could've been worse." Alec abandons his tools and points for me to sit on the back of the ATV while he busts open the first aid kit.

"I know. I wasn't thinking."

Alec wipes a disinfectant pad across the wound and I wince. That stings worse than the barb I jammed into my finger. We're stringing a new part of barbed wire fence and we're deep in the acreage of the ranch. I should have had my gloves on, he's right. But I've been distracted since I saw Colby for the first time last weekend and I wrapped my hand around the wire without thinking. It's a good thing I only caught my finger.

"You need to be thinking out here, Dante. We don't need hospital visits." He applies an antibiotic ointment and a Band-Aid with military precision. Satisfied with his doctoring, he motions to the gloves in my pockets. "Now put them on until we're done here."

I do as I'm told and return to my section, working until we finish one part and move to the next.

Alec parks the vehicle close to our next task and silently we unload the materials. We need to replace a few fence posts. I'm ready to go, but before we begin, he sighs and asks me to sit on the gate of the ATV again.

"Listen, Dan sort of filled me in on what went down on Sunday. I didn't want to say anything earlier. I was still upset that I lost Sally." He removes his cowboy hat and swipes at his hair before placing it back. "But it's obviously bothering you and I know you don't have anyone to talk to. We've worked together now almost every day for a few weeks and I like you. You don't have to trust me, but I'm offering that to you. To be a friend you can trust if you need one."

My body trembles. "Why?" I croak. "Why would you do that?"

He studies the sky for a moment, the breeze flutters his hair that pokes out from under his hat and I wonder if he's all alone too.

"Because when I was your age, I would've loved to have someone to talk to. Dan's built up a good thing here. All he does is help and give and as his right-hand man for the past few years, it rubs off on you. He tries not to get too attached, but when he met Martin that all went out the window. Now he wants to love everyone and everything as hard as he possibly can. Because now he knows what he was missing all those years alone." Again he looks off into the distance and I don't know if I should talk now or bite my tongue.

He turns to me again. "So I guess to answer your question, it's because I know the loneliness you feel and I'd like to make it easier if I can."

The early June sun shines on my face when I tilt my head back. The sky is clear and blue, only a few puffy clouds floating by. I thank whoever might be listening that put me in the path of all the people I've met since I served my time. I'm not good enough to deserve all this good will, but I'm also only human and I grab onto it with both hands.

"I was seventeen when I fell in love with Colby. I didn't act on it for an entire year because I wasn't sure if he felt the same. When I was eighteen I let him kiss me and everything changed. I knew true happiness when he was around. He's sunshine and hope and everything I ever wanted." A few geese fly overhead and I focus on the sounds of their wings while Alec sits and listens.

"We had plans to tell our parents right after graduation, before we went to college. He was taking some kind of business course. He wanted to open a business one day. So we could work together and never be apart, was what he'd say." I swallow back the thickness in my throat. "I was going to take accounting so I could do something to help him. He was the people person between us. I was the guy who never opened his mouth because I was usually wrong."

Alec still remains silent, but he's watching me and it makes it almost too hard to continue.

"Colby loved me anyway, though, and he showed me all the time. Told me, too. And that all fell apart because I let us be careless. I wasn't paying attention and... and... the secret was out."

"You weren't out?" Alec asks softly.

I shake my head hard. "Yes, well, no. Our family knew we were gay, but not with each other. It was, uh, family issues. My dad... he gave me an ultimatum. I can't say he gave me a choice. There was only one option that was acceptable. So I left to save Colby from that. I left. For him."

I'm not going to cry to a cowboy. This is bullshit. Launching off the back of the ATV, I march towards the supplies for fencing and grab the auger to start a new post hole. But it's extra heavy right now in my arms and my vision is blurring. Then the equipment is on the ground and I'm being pulled into the arms of my new friend whether I want to or not.

"I left for him. It was all for him."

All the rage and tears I've been holding onto for five years comes flooding out as I crumble into the arms of my coworker and I guess, my new friend. I never meant to break like this to anyone, ever. After five years of never showing emotion or giving anything away, I apparently reached my limit. Alec says nothing, only holds onto me while I let it all out and I feel like an overextended rubber band.

I just want my damn life back.

He hands me a handkerchief and I mop up the tears and snot.

"Thank you for everything. It's been a long time since I've had a friend who would listen."

"You're welcome and if you need to unload again, come to me. Nobody needs to carry that all the time."

With ease, he scoops the auger up and we work to drill a new post hole and install the post. We work in silence as we always have these past few weeks. But I'm acutely aware of the change in our dynamic and I'm thankful for it.

No one has been on my side since, well since Colby, and I really miss that. If Alec is offering me his ear, I could really use some advice.

When we're done with the fencing and back at the ranch, he invites me to his cabin. He lives in the foreman's quarters, a small old style farmhouse set back from the main house. It used to be the original homestead, and Dan first lived here while building the new house he now occupies. Alec's home has been remodelled and it's like something out of a magazine for Better Homes and Gardens. It's so cozy and bright that just setting foot inside makes you smile. He even has plants on the window sills and hanging in a few places. It's a dream.

We still have work to do, but he wants to change the bandage on my finger and he offered me a cold drink with leftovers. He may just be offering to be polite, but either way, a hot meal is a hot meal. And eating it with someone who cares and already saw me break down gives me a feeling I can't put a name to.

When Alec very gently unwraps my finger and cleans it again for me, I ask for his opinion.

"I didn't handle what I said to Colby very well. He was actually talking to Babe about me when I found him. I wasn't expecting to hear him talk about me like that and I invited myself into the conversation. It's not how I wanted my first meeting with him to go. Do you think I should try to explain again? Should I find him and ask to talk now?"

Alec finishes applying my new Band-Aid and leans back in the chair.

"I think he deserves an explanation if you have one, but you need to be prepared that he may not like or want to hear what you have to say. And if that's the case, are you prepared for him to push you away?"

"Well he did once, right? He didn't stay to talk last week, he just left in anger and I get that. I do. But I hope he'd allow me to explain again and have a chance to at least be in his life. If not as his boyfriend then as a friend."

Alec nods and snaps the first aid kit closed.

"My suggestion to you would be to remain cautious and ask him how he wants to talk. In a public place or private, with friends or without. He needs to know he has allies around because, like it or not, it sounds like you're the bad guy right now." He shifts in his chair and leans forward. "But I do have to ask, why wasn't your family communicating? How come he's been left in the dark for so long?"

Because I made a deal with the devil, that's why.

"I can't tell you everything because Colby needs to hear that first. They're actually part of the problem and he doesn't even know yet."

Alec checks his phone. "It's 2:30 P.M. on a Thursday. The candy store is open late Thursdays and if you want to borrow my shower, consider yourself off for the rest of the day."

My heart pounds in my chest. "Really? Uh, thank you. I'll grab my things from the car. But, is it okay to go to the store? Do you think he'll get mad?"

He shrugs. "I think he'll be mad no matter what. But Landon won't let you in the apartment, of that much I'm sure."

Jealousy rears its head. I'd never allowed myself to consider what my feelings would be if Colby had moved on. "Oh, he has a boyfriend then. Maybe I should let it all be. He deserves happiness. I don't want to upset that."

I don't want to come between him and anyone else. I do want him in my life, though, and if I need to step aside and not be involved romantically, then it will have to be that way.

Alec booms laughter. "No, you can relax. Landon is his best friend and they live together. He's very protective."

I laugh nervously, "Great. Protective best friend."

Alec smiles and claps a hand on my shoulder.

"Clear the air, Dante. Do that and go from there. Just be prepared to give him time if needed."

I guess this is it, then.

Chapter 8

Colby

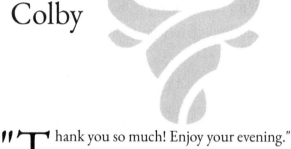

"Thank you so much! Enjoy your evening."

The last group of tourists leave the shop and my sales are loving the start of tourist season. In fact, I'm thinking I should look at providing some souvenirs in the shop to go along with all the candy. It could be a nice bump in income to help fund the ice cream bar I want to add.

"Ah, decisions. I'll have to meet with my accountant about that. I'm not a numbers guy."

I start my nightly walk around, straightening the product and returning misplaced items, humming along to the catchy pop song on the radio.

The door opens to another short burst of rock music and there's nothing but silence. No giggling adults at the sound of the doorbell or kids rushing off to check out the self-serve jelly beans. Without even turning around, I know who it is. There's a change in the air and the hairs on my arms stand up. His voice never failed to make me shiver. It's so very different from when we were teenagers, but still so... Dante.

"Please don't make me go, Colby. I wanted to come and talk and I don't know where you live. Please, just give me a chance to talk."

Turning around from the display I was tidying, my heart trips at the sight of the man who still holds it. After I spent an entire day in bed and calling in my back up staff to work this week, I made a decision.

"I think we should talk as well."

We stand there like a pair of deer caught in the headlights, neither of us wanting to look away. Part of me still doesn't believe he's even real. To have him standing in my candy store after all this time does funny things to my heart.

"I, ah, I brought you something." Dante opens his hand and unwraps the piece of tissue surrounding the pink candy stick and I hang my head when I see what it is.

"Pulling out all the stops right away aren't you?" I allow my lips to tilt in a small smile before meeting his face again.

"I couldn't take the chance of you saying no again. You never turn down a Lik-a-Stix."

I stare into the deep brown eyes that have haunted every waking moment of my life since he left.

"Because I could never turn you down, Dante. It was always you."

It took a lot for me to admit to myself this week that I wanted to hear what he said, no matter how angry I was. I wanted to know why he hurt me so badly, even if it hurt me all over again to hear it. I just had to either close the door with his answers or maybe, just maybe I could leave it open and we could find our way back to each other.

I take the piece of candy from him along with the tissue and place it on the counter.

"Let me lock up and I have a back office. We can talk there."

He stuffs his hands in his jeans and in a blink he's transformed back to the nineteen-year-old boy I loved. With his molten brown eyes and easy smile whenever I entered the room. He'd stuff his hands in his pockets when our parents were around because he always wanted to touch me. To hold my hand or run his fingers through my hair, anything to connect with me. Even that subtle little touch with his pinky against mine while we cleaned up after supper in the kitchen. Inexplicably drawn to each other, we were.

I swallow hard when I notice him watching me and my stomach flip flops under his gaze. The guy disappears without a trace and he still gets me with a single glance and a Fun Dip stick.

I flick on the closed sign and motion for him to follow me to my office.

"Can I offer you anything? I have ginger ale and granola bars."

He looks around my office with the small loveseat and fuzzy blanket. There's no desk. If I do paperwork here it's on a small pop up table. Even the light back here is low and not fluorescent. Dante notices.

"Is this your room in case one of your headaches comes while at work?" He smooths a hand over the blanket with a sad frown. "Did you ever get answers about that?"

I sit on the other end of the loveseat and pull my knees to my chest.

"Chronic migraines. My mom fought for an MRI and we had one. No tumours or anything abnormal."

"Thank god. I... I often thought about you and hoped it wasn't anything serious. I still remember that time you were so violently sick and I didn't know what to do."

"I remember. You thought I ate bad tuna."

We both laugh softly at the memory, but the laughter dies just as fast as it came.

"They often get more intense when I'm stressed." My voice drops to a whisper and I nudge my socked foot into his thigh. "They got a lot worse when you disappeared. That's when I had the scan, my mom was frantic."

"Colby... I..."

He swallows and I force myself to look into his handsome face. The sharp lines of his jaw pop with tension and there's a small scar on his chin he didn't have before. "Why did you leave me, Dante? I've not lived properly since you left, you know. When you left, the hole was too big for me."

His dark eyelashes kiss his cheeks as he closes his eyes. Hanging his head, I know it hurts him to hear me say that. He was always one to struggle with words and feelings, but when he found the right words, he never wasted a single one. He had to have known I'd say something like that, though, and it's the only way I know how to speak. My feelings are out there all the time.

"Did my dad even say anything? Or try to find me?"

"All he told us was that you ran away and he thought you might have tried to find your mom's family, but nobody had heard from you. He said he filed a missing person report and it was all he could do." Swallowing hard, I remember the day an officer came to the house to question me. "When an officer came to talk to me, he didn't seem to care either."

Dante finally allows himself to touch my foot and when he does a bolt of electricity shoots through me. Nothing has changed that way. This man is still the one who can turn on every nerve inside me with one tiny touch. He puffs out a shaky breath and I know he feels it too. There's no way, in my heart of hearts I can't not love him. No one has come close to connecting with me the way he does.

But I need to know why he'd hurt me like that.

"I didn't want to go. You have to believe that, please. I never contacted you because... I've been in jail, Colby."

I can't even form words. My beautiful, sweet and kind Dante has been in jail? Impossible.

"I, how... how come we didn't know? Your dad would've heard and told us! I would've visited. I would've helped!"

God I would have been there every day for him no matter what.

"It's not that easy, Colbs. I couldn't do that to you."

Popping off the sofa, I pace, spearing my hands in my hair and pulling hard enough to make it hurt.

"But you could leave me alone for five fucking years wondering why I made you leave? You preferred to let me suffer not knowing if you were alive, dead or just not wanting to be in my life? What the fuck, Dante? They have phones in prison! Why didn't you call?"

I turn and stare at him with clenched jaw and fists. And his downcast eyes break me. Again I'm softening for this man, even after he hasn't explained himself to me.

His broken voice has me rushing to him, because even though I've been shattered for years, I want to keep Dante whole.

"I want to tell you everything, Colby. I really do, but I can't. At least not yet. I need time." He reaches for my hand and I allow it. He pulls me to him and I crumble. I fall into him and hug him so tight it's a wonder he can breathe. He buries his face in my neck and his warm breath skates across my skin. "I've missed you so much." The crack in his voice wavers and he squeezes me harder. "You just have to believe me that I never wanted to hurt you, but I had no choice."

God, how I've missed this. Him holding me and making me feel safe, but the betrayal I feel still sits like the proverbial elephant in the room. Why? We knew everything about each other. We shared everything and he's keeping the one thing I need the most from him right now.

"D... I never stopped loving you." With regret, I force myself off him and study his face. "I want to pretend all is well and you're back and just go on how we used to be. I really do. So fucking much it keeps me up at night, and sometimes it's hard to breathe knowing you're not there."

"Please... "

Hugging my arms around my body, the familiar throb in my temple picks up and I can't believe the day I've been wishing for is finally here and I might be wishing it never came. Because healing once is hard enough, twice is going to be a challenge.

"What you don't know, Dante, is last week I made the choice to move on with my life. I chose to move on and when you showed up at the ranch, I had such mixed emotions that I doubted my decision. Because I've never wanted anyone but you, and suddenly you were there in front of me." I have to look away from him. His puppy dog eyes are breaking my heart.

"But... I can't just accept that answer. I can't. Because it's not enough. And if you can't trust me to tell me why you couldn't call me for five years or send an email or anything, then how can I just go back to trusting that you won't disappear again?" I swallow the massive lump in my throat back. "I love you so much I've never stopped thinking of you. And if you can't tell me everything and be truthful, I just can't accept that. Because if this were to happen again and you disappeared? I don't think I could make it through that again. I really don't."

Dante hangs his head and my shoulders sag with the weight of the silence in the room. He finally stands, and when he lifts his head tears have stained his cheeks. He never cries, but I can't do this. Not unless he's willing to tell me everything.

"You just have to trust me, like you always did, Colbs. I just... I need more time. I'm still me and I'll never let anything happen to you. But I understand why you'd not want me around, I just don't want to accept it."

"Then don't accept it and tell me what happened. Don't leave us like this after all this time," I beg.

"I can't, Colbs. I don't know when, but I can't right now."

My body trembles when he pauses next to me and places a kiss on my cheek, lingering for a little longer than needed.

His hoarse whisper breaks me all over again, "You'll always be a part of me, Colbs. Don't ever think I don't love you, but some details you can't ever know, and if losing you to protect you is what I have to do, then I'll do it until I die."

Dante doesn't look back, and leaves me standing in my office as he lets himself out the front door. The riff of rock music isn't one I want to hear, and I barely manage to make it to the front to flip the lock again. With tears blurring my vision, I stumble back to my office and collapse on the love seat.

Too broken to even call Landon.

Too hurt to care if anyone is worried, and too damn sorry for myself to do anything but curl up in a ball and hope all the pain magically disappears during sleep.

Chapter 9

Dante

"Hey Dante! What do you know about llamas?"

Dan has just returned from a rescue pick up, and he's backed a small trailer up to one of the barns. Yesterday I worked to fabricate a makeshift pen for a llama that needed care and I've been waiting for him to return. All Dan would say was that a llama needed special care and I was to be ready. I haven't researched llamas or anything, although I should've, to distract myself.

"Uh, not a lot but I can learn. What do you need from me?"

He adjusts his cowboy hat with a grin. "Well, first off, a llama wrangler."

There's no way this is going to be your regular old run-of-the-mill animal unloading. I may have only been on the job for a month now, but I know my boss well enough to know he's not being transparent. His shit-eating grin is also an indication.

He peeks through the door of the horse trailer and a high pitched hum followed by the thumping of feet fills the air, and he chuckles.

"It took two of us to get her in there. Two very large men, Dante. And the darn thing spits like you wouldn't believe. But she's scared and doesn't understand what's happening."

I can relate to that. I don't understand most things these days either. Except for being here for Colby and hoping he lets me back in.

More stomping sounds from the trailer.

"Uh, so what can you tell me about her and how can I help?"

Dan takes a coil of rope from the back of his truck before scratching his head again. "Well, this is Mittens and she's a llama who has what you'd call an identity crisis."

"Uh, say what now?"

He chuckles as he slips the rope around the door handle of the trailer. "The farmer's son called me when his dad was distraught because Mittens wasn't eating. They said they spoke to a vet but didn't get much help so they called me." I watch him stretch the rope over to the barn and nod to himself as he ties the other end to a post. "Turns out it's not a vet issue. Well it is, but not the normal kind. Mittens needs an animal behaviourist. She needs therapy, I guess."

Is there even such a thing for animals?

"I'm afraid I don't know anything about animal therapy. What's her issue?"

Dan motions for me to help him lift a gate and we create a chute to lead Mittens straight into the pen I built for her. I'm still perplexed as to what I'm expected to do with this llama. Especially if she needs therapy. I probably need some myself and I'm definitely not qualified to pull up a chair with a llama and have her tell me about her childhood.

We step aside as he opens the trailer door. "She thinks she's a cat."

I don't have much time to digest that nugget of information because Mittens bolts out of the trailer like her ass is on fire, making a weird humming noise and spitting everywhere. A gob of spit hits my arm and Mittens races into the barn stall.

"Hurry, close up the gates so she can't run out of the stall!"

Dan and I hurry to make sure Mittens can't bolt right back out and once we're certain she's secure, I turn to Dan.

"So, I'm gonna need some more guidance and explanation here. How does a llama think it's a cat?"

Mittens has retreated to the farthest corner of the pen and is squishing herself into the corner in an attempt to become invisible. My heart breaks for her. I don't know how a llama feels, but I know how I felt in a strange and new place. One with fences and doors to keep me in and nobody to understand me.

Maybe me and Mittens have more in common than I first thought. I didn't think I was a cat when I was placed in prison, but I did think I was someone else. Someone who was mistakenly put there, and I wanted to bury my head just like her. I was just as scared. There were new people and new rules and it smelled funny.

Yep, me and Mittens really do have a lot in common.

Dan rests his arms on the stall next to me. "Theory is that she was a baby llama with a barn cat. The cat was more of a feral barn cat and she copied the cat's behaviour. She'd run from humans and make sounds if they got too close. She doesn't eat from the trough.

I think it was one of those times where the timing was right and with no mother she imprinted on the cat. Mittens was taken from her mom too early, I think."

Humming noises still sound intermittently from Mittens and I already know I'll do whatever I have to so this animal can at least accept it's a llama and be sociable. I don't know if animals can sense if other animals are different, but I don't want her to be like that. Even if she still thinks she's a cat, I want her to be a llama-cat that likes people.

Dan nudges me with his shoulder. "I think you're perfect for this. I still need you around the ranch for chores and definitely for the haying season, but Mittens I trust with you. She needs a patient person with a kind heart to help her."

I pull my hat down tighter. "Some people might argue with that person being me."

He shrugs. "Then those people don't know you." He strolls to the rope left on the ground and winds it around his hand as he talks. "Martin is making early dinner tonight. If you want to join us you're welcome. Just come up to the house when you're done."

Dan jumps in the truck after securing the trailer doors and drives it off, leaving me alone with a scared and confused llama.

"I don't even have a phone to google anything to help you, girl."

Movement at the barn door draws my attention. Colby stands there, cowboy hat pulled low and his hands in his back pockets.

"We have to stop sneaking up on each other in barns." He removes his phone from a pocket and holds it out. "I have something for Google if you need it. I'm taking a short ride and there's no cell service there anyway. You're welcome to use it."

Maybe this is the first step to us bridging the gap I left and he's trying to forgive me. Or maybe it's Colby just being the kind person he always is.

"It's not Sunday," I say, instead of anything remotely intelligent, and he smiles.

"No, it's not. I try to come out at least once during the week when the winter is over." He looks over his shoulder and into the late afternoon sun. "It's a nice day. I figured I'd take Babe for a stroll and do some thinking."

I want to ask him so bad if he's thinking of me, but I don't. I can wish for it, though.

"If you don't mind, yeah, I could use your phone. That would really help, thank you." My fingers brush his as he passes it to me and our eyes meet, but he quickly looks away.

"I'll be back in a few hours. Will I find you here or do you want to leave my phone somewhere? I don't know your schedule... "

Colby shoves his hands back in his pockets and I stammer a response. "I, uh, no, I'll be here. With the llama. Like not *with* with the llama, but I'll be here." I point my finger to the ground and roll my own eyes at how completely lame the gesture is.

He holds back a laugh and I feel lighter to know he's willing to be in the same space with me, at least. And smiling. When he turns to leave, I drop my attention to the phone to find the screen lock is on.

"Colby! What's your password for the screen lock?" I call after him.

Turning back, he assesses me and in a quiet voice says, "A day we'll both never forget."

He leaves me then and I watch him mount Babe and saunter out to the meadow. My gaze stays locked on him until he's far enough away and I can no longer make out his silhouette.

"Mittens, you think he's been using that as his code all this time?"

She twitches an ear but doesn't turn her head. Not that I expected her to or anything, but might as well try to get her used to me.

My fingers punch in the date I left, 0531 and the screen opens while I sink onto a bale of hay. For five years he's reminded himself everyday of what's probably the worst day of his life. It was the worst day of mine, that's for sure. I use the date for codes too, but it's because I want to remember I still have something to keep me moving forward. But only I know why I left. He thinks I abandoned him, so why would he use the same code to bring back bad memories?

"I think I need to consider telling him everything, Mittens. I can't wait until it's all sorted and wrapped in a little bow."

Before I google "llamas and behaviour issues," I first look up the number to the crown attorney's office and scribble it on a receipt from my car.

With any luck, the same man who told me to call him when I was sentenced will still be willing to listen.

Chapter 10

Colby

"I can't stand looking at all these estimates and cost comparisons and contractor jargon."

I growl, tossing the folder onto the coffee table and Landon snatches it to flip through my mess.

"You could probably ask Dan to help you. He had that new barn built last year and he used one of these contractors. Or maybe someone else at the ranch could help... "

Landon purposely leaves the words hanging while pretending to still examine the boring estimates. He knows the plan Dante had and how he was good at this kind of stuff.

"Am I stupid for wanting to ask him? To let him back in? Because I've been thinking about it far too much. And I lent him my phone the other day." I allow a smile to form thinking of him with that poor llama. "And I was thinking about what my mom said last time she was here, remember? She said by forgiving we can move on. Maybe I should listen."

Although I don't want to move on and leave him behind. I want to move ahead and bring him with me. I know I told him I couldn't unless he told me why he left, but it's not that easy. Seeing him at the ranch now makes it even harder because he smiles and says hello to me. I watch him work with the llama and my horse is always happy to see him.

Animals' reactions to people can't be ignored. They are the best judges of character.

Landon flops back and takes a sip of his smoothie. It's a Friday evening and we've stayed in together for once. He didn't have a shift at the gym and his courses are now over for the summer. Instead of going out like twenty-somethings should, we opted to stay in, order pizza and watch YouTube episodes of *How'd They Do That*.

It's a glamorous life.

"Forgiveness looks different for everyone, Colby. Is asking him to help you read blueprints and contractors estimates forgiveness to you? Or is it just you needing something to break the ice and get talking?"

"I'd feel pretty wrong if I just asked his opinion and then told him to fuck off. I'd have to forgive him to even ask."

He rips a slice of pizza from the box and takes a bite. "Do you want me to be blunt?"

I snort. "You're my best friend, I always expect you to be."

He chews and swallows before setting his slice back down. "I've known you since college. I may never have met you if Dante would have stuck to your plan, you know. Without what happened to you two, I'd never have met you. But I'm selfish like that and while I hate that you went through all the pain of losing him, I'm happy you did because I got to know you."

"You can't miss what you don't know, though."

He shakes his head. "You're missing the point. What happened to you both shaped who you are today. It wasn't pleasant but there's good in there somewhere. This whole thing that you still don't know why or have answers to? He did it for you and for some reason he doesn't want to tell you, but... he's obviously not lying. I mean, I haven't really got to meet him and grill him like a proper best friend should, but from what you've told me, he's a good guy." He picks up his pizza again. "And you're not over him. Even when you said you were letting go, you weren't. Because he's so much a part of you, you don't know how to let go."

Landon keeps eating while I stare at my best friend. He's definitely right about me not letting go. I wanted to be strong and close the door, but there's that voice inside me that keeps getting louder saying to open it and let him back in. And I'm starting to think that voice knows something I don't.

"When did you get so wise?"

He snorts, "Tell that to my teachers, they'd disagree with that."

Landon's right. The voice in my head is right. My damn horse is right.

"I know I said we'd stay in together, but... "

He waves his hand in the air, shooing me away. "Go. It's fine. I'll be here."

I don't even know where to look for Dante or where he's staying but the town isn't that big. How hard can it be?

"Thanks, Lan. I've got my phone and I'll call if I need you."

Stuffing my feet in my sneakers, I grab my car keys and set off to find Dante.

Turns out finding Dante in a small town is harder than I thought.

I drove around the streets I knew with apartment buildings. I didn't see his car, but that wouldn't matter because how would I know what building he's in without knocking on every single door?

I also drove by a few of the rooming houses and even the youth shelter in town. It's for teens mostly, but I don't think they'd turn away anyone if they truly needed it. But I've been searching for ninety minutes and need a break.

My tires crunch on the gravel of the parking lot at the recreation area in town, Dogwood Pond. It's far too late to consider taking the hiking path up to our spot, but I can still stare out at the water for a while. It's early in the spring and while the trees are leafed out, most of the gardens are only just starting to grow. But there's a bench by the water and the gentle sound of waves lapping at the shoreline always soothes the soul.

When I start to walk towards the path to the pond's edge, movement out of the corner of my eye draws my attention. A car is parked far into the corner of the lot where the lot lighting doesn't quite reach and a figure moves. The more I watch, the more it feels familiar and when they open the car door, the light from inside illuminates their profile and my breath hitches.

My feet move on their own accord across the parking lot until he turns when he hears my footsteps.

"Oh, hey Colby." His shoulders drop and he moves in front of the open car door, but I've seen enough.

"Dante... are you... were you going to sleep in your car?"

Rubbing the back of his neck he nods. "Uh, yep. This is my home. It's not much right now, but I have nowhere else to go."

My heart drops knowing he's been sleeping and living out of his car since he was released.

"Why didn't you tell me?"

He shrugs, keeping his eyes on his feet.

"You have enough to deal with seeing me again, I wasn't about to tell you I'm homeless at the same time."

I should've known he had nowhere to go, hell I even drove by shelters tonight, but I didn't think he'd be sleeping in a car.

"I'd have helped if I knew, Dante. I'm not heartless."

I never could be when it comes to you.

"I know, but I can't ask you for that kind of help. Not now."

I stare at him in the moonlight and the low, yellow glow from the car's interior lights. The tiredness, the bone deep sadness and the reality of his situation are far more visible now than they've ever been. His brown eyes don't shine like they used to, and his shoulders slump. I've been a fool, with reason, but still a fool.

"You're not asking me. I'm telling you, come home with me." His eyebrows shoot up and I know he wants to protest, but I stop him.

"Please, Dante. I've been looking for you and I'm not letting you stay here. Come home with me."

He chews his lip while he scuffs the toe of his sneaker in the dirt.

"Is it... will it be awkward to have me around if I go with you?"

"It'll be more awkward to know you're out here alone. I can't let you do that." I scuff at the same ground with my sneaker and touch his foot. "And I want us to talk. I want us to... I don't know yet, but I want you to.... " My throat is thick and I swallow hard. "I want you in my life."

He clears his throat, looking away as he answers. "I'd like that."

"Good. Okay, uh, follow me home? I'm at sixty-three Sandy Lane in case we get split up."

I walk back to my car and with shaking hands I start it and wait for him to drive across the lot. Once I know he's ready, I point my car in the direction of home and obsessively check my rear view mirror to make sure he's following me. When I finally do pull into my driveway it's a miracle I made it without an accident. I didn't want to see his car disappear and spent more time looking behind than in front of me. Believe me, I'm aware of the irony.

I motion for Dante to park behind me and wait for him.

"Do you need help bringing anything inside?"

He removes a backpack from the trunk with a sad smile. "All I have fits in here." He smacks the bag with a sad smile. "Unless you want me to bring in my blankets?"

I shake my head. "No, we have spares. Come on."

Landon and I rent the main floor of a bungalow and as we approach the entrance, Dante grabs my arm.

"Does your roommate know I'm coming? I don't want to impose, Colby, at all." He rubs his neck again, "And I heard he's protective of you."

It breaks my heart he's still not thinking of himself in any way, but that's the Dante I always knew and I want him back.

"He knows. He told me to go find you, actually." I take his hand in mine. "And he's a big teddy bear. He won't cause trouble."

"Am I going to like him?"

"A thousand percent, now quit stalling."

We step into the entrance and Landon is still in the living room, feet on the coffee table and watching TV. When he hears us he immediately stands when he notices I'm not alone.

"Hey Lan, I should've called, but ah, I found him."

Landon gives Dante a once over before extending his hand. "Nice to meet you... finally."

He takes Landon's hand and stands tall. It's a bit like bringing home a boyfriend to meet the parents and I have to hide my smile. "Thank you for being okay with having me here. I can't tell you how much I appreciate it."

"Don't tell me, tell Colby." He cleans up the cups and pizza box from the coffee table. "I'll leave you two alone. If you need me I'm in my room."

Dante stands frozen in place, unsure of what to do or say.

"Make yourself comfortable, I'll get something to drink. Do you still like ginger ale? I have some if you'd like."

He drops his pack at the end of the sofa and sits. "I still drink it, but I don't need anything, thanks."

I take a seat on the opposite end of the sofa and we both try to talk at once.

"I miss you - "

"I'm sorry - "

We laugh together and he motions for me to go first.

"I miss you, a lot. And I wasn't fair maybe, asking you to leave like I did. So, maybe we could start over?"

"I'm sorry for not giving you much information that day, but I will in time. I've just... I've had to check a lot of things and I'm still waiting on answers and I'll tell you everything. I promise, Colbs."

Chewing on my lip I nod. "I know what you searched on my phone the other day. It wasn't just llamas."

He sucks in a breath and I wait to hear what he has to say.

"I'm checking on some things before I tell you, but I called and spoke to the guy who handled my trial. He told me to call him when I was released if I changed my mind."

Inching closer to him, I take his hand in mine. "Changed your mind about what?"

He puffs out a breath and tugs me closer. "I served time because I didn't give the prosecutors the names they wanted." He rushes on, "There's a reason I didn't then, okay? Yes I could've and I'd have been let go, but then I would've had the possibility of never seeing you again if I did. So that was off the table and I said I had three years to think about it."

When someone tells you they went to prison, that they served time simply for the chance to get to see you again, that's not something to easily overlook. As much as I want to know all the answers right now, he's given me a little bit and I'd be a cold hearted fool to not accept it.

"D, will I get to know what happened? All of it?"

He makes the final tug and I crawl on top of him. His hands, now roughened by farm labour, smooth up my back, just like he used to when we'd sit together in our short pieces of extended time together.

"I'll tell you everything, just give me time to make sure it's okay."

My hands fist his shirt and I stare into his dark eyes. "And you're not going to disappear again?"

"Not unless someone drags me kicking and screaming. Even then, I'll fight to be here and never let you go." He passes the back of his hand over my cheek. "You've only grown more beautiful since I've been away. Thinking of you is what gave me a reason to keep waking up every day."

I shiver at his gentle touch. "I've only been thinking of how horrible I've felt without you and I've never considered what you may have been feeling. I was angry you didn't say goodbye and once I got over the anger, all I did was grieve for you. I just wanted to have you back. Whether it was for a last goodbye or a new hello, I just needed you."

He swallows hard and his voice is hoarse when he speaks, "I'm here now, and I don't want to say goodbye, Colbs. Not ever."

I press my lips to his and revel in everything Dante. The feel of his warm skin against mine and the low buzz, like an electric current, that always seems to pass between us. The rightness of how it feels to be pressed into him as our tongues tangle and my fingers card through his hair. What is it about his hair sliding through my fingers that sends goosebumps racing up my arms?

He sits up, pulling me into him.

I punch my hips forward and grind on his lap, drawing gasps from both of us until I lean back, panting.

"Can you stay with me tonight? I don't think I can bear having you sleep on the couch."

For several moments neither of us say anything, we stay like that with him rubbing my back and my face buried in his neck, my fingers tangled in his hair. It doesn't matter about the sex, I just don't want to let him go.

"Anything you want, lead the way."

Chapter 11

Dante

Colby closes the door to his bedroom and switches on a lamp near his bed. A quick glance up confirms he removed the overhead light bulb. He did that when we still lived at home and the headaches started. Sometimes low lighting helped. He stands in the middle of the room, but I'm still frozen by the door. I know he invited me here but I'm all mixed up inside and I don't know what to do.

He peels his shirt off over his head and tosses it in the corner before moving to the button of his jeans. His eyes never leave mine and while I know what's expected to happen, I'm nervous and Colby picks up on that.

"No expectations, D. We can just sleep together and nothing else. I just don't want to be away from you anymore."

He steps closer and lays a hand on my chest. I want to do everything and nothing at the same time. I take his hand in mine and feather a kiss on his wrist. This man is the only one I've ever loved. I can trust him with anything.

I puff out a shaky breath. "I... fuck this is awkward. Uh, there's been no one else since you."

His lips part as he processes my words. "Like, ever?"

"Never."

He takes my hands in his with a squeeze.

"You haven't been with anyone for five years?"

"Well, the first two years I couldn't even think of being with anyone but you. In prison, that's just a hard no. I was fortunate that way and I'll spare you the details. So, no. It's only been you."

His face softens more as he tugs my shirt free from my pants. "It's just me, D. If you're nervous I get it. But I'm still that guy who could kiss you for hours behind the barn because I loved the way your hair felt in my hands. Or the way your hands could make me feel like I was a fragile treasure." He drops a kiss over my heart, "But mostly, I'm just me and you're still the person for me."

When he mentions behind the barn, my heart races because I remember those times. And I can taste it right now. The hopefulness of our youth and the unmatched lust of two teenagers. But mostly, the way Colby could make me forget all of the day's problems and make me feel like I was the king of everything.

I want to feel that way again. Pulling him into me, I walk him back until I press him against the wall and a warm breath from his lips puffs across my too hot skin. He buries his fingers in my hair with a groan and my hands drift. My fingers find every new dip and valley on his lithe body and his kisses steal the air from my lungs. But he doesn't need to steal it, I'd give him my last breath in a heartbeat if he needed it.

His nails rake across my scalp and my nerves have settled now that I've found the familiarity of him again. I've never wanted anyone like I've wanted Colby.

"Naked?" I mumble against his lips as I try to tug his pants down.

"That would help." He breathes back and we break apart to shuck the rest of our clothes before tumbling on the bed together.

My elbow cracks the side of the bedside table, "Ow, fuck."

"You okay?" His brows furrow.

"My first sex injury. Should I be concerned?"

"Nah, I got you."

Colby places a tender kiss on my elbow and blows gently over it and I damn near combust.

"Better?" he whispers.

"Can you do that in other places?"

With a sly grin he does the same on my collar bone, then my chest and then my navel. Every time he places a kiss he swirls his tongue and then blows on it.

I grab at his shoulders. "C'mere, please."

He slides back up my body and I take his face in my hands. Gorgeous blue eyes stare back at me and his parted lips are slick with saliva. I kiss his forehead. "I think if you put your mouth on me any lower it'll all be over."

"We have all the time ever to get to that. But you know what we can do now? What we always wanted to?" He slides off me and lays on his side, pulling me over with a leg across my hip so we face each other. "We never got to lay in a bed like this and just be. We never ever spent time in bed together for anything."

He's right. It was kisses and hand jobs in the darkness of the barn or in the little grove at the look out. It was all we had and we looked forward to the day we could be with each other like this. Now it's here and I'm almost afraid to do anything. I feel like an awkward teenager again. My hands slide down his smooth skin and I give his ass a firm squeeze.

"Do you happen to keep lube in that dangerous night stand of yours?"

"I do." He grins and places a kiss on my lips before rolling over me to reach the stand. He straddles me with a shy grin and reaches into the drawer. When he reaches for the drawer, the soft heat of his cock brushes mine and I hold his hips in place with a quiet curse.

"Fuck, Colby. Don't judge me when I shoot off in record time, okay? I'm all kinds of turned on and overwhelmed right now. You feel far too good."

Which is probably an understatement, but I don't want to be that guy who cries during sex because he has so many *feelings*. Not only is it a turn off, but I want Colby to come and be satisfied. Attempting anything other than a handy right now is most likely a bad idea if I want him to have any kind of satisfaction here.

"Don't think I'm not in the same boat. It's been too long and you're the only one I've ever wanted." He squirts lube in his hand, slicking up both our cocks with a moan. "You're the only one I ever think of."

He rocks gently and grips our dicks together in a delicious slide and my eyes never leave his face. The pink flush to his pale skin is beyond gorgeous as he drops his head forward with a groan. Other than gripping his hips so tight I'll leave fingerprints behind, I let Colby lead. His free hand presses hard in the middle of my chest, like he's pinning me to the mattress with everything he's got as he ruts against me.

A low moan fills the room and it's me. Colby's eyes shoot up to mine and he rocks faster through his slippery hold. The fire burning in his eyes isn't one I remember from when we were kids. Maybe it's a part of the growing up process and the hard years I put us through, but it's not just sex addled lust. It's more and it makes my chest ache to have it aimed at me.

My body shakes and shudders like an old car left in the cold too long, and the cum pours out of me like a faucet.

"Colby... oh fuck..."

He doesn't stop until his own load mixes with mine and he collapses on me with a low groan. His heart pounds so hard I feel it next to mine as I wrap my arms tight around him.

"D?"

"Yeah?"

"I think my brain melted and I can't feel my legs."

I laugh softly and kiss his jaw. "You're talking so the brain must be okay. As for the legs, let me help you." He sits up and I wince with the sticky pull on my belly hairs. "Jesus, there's enough cum here to spackle a hole in the wall and have some left over."

"No wonder I can't feel my legs." He laughs and I help him up, massaging his legs with a grin.

"How about you show me the bathroom, we get cleaned up and fall asleep together?"

"I'd like that. The bathroom is across the hall, we'll streak over."

A laugh barks out and he smiles at me and fuck have I missed his shining face. "Now you're a streaker, I've missed a lot since I've been gone."

He peeks out the door and reaches back to grab my hand.

"And we've got a lifetime to catch up."

With a tug he pulls me after him to the bathroom and it's the most free I've felt in my entire life.

The early morning sun isn't quite up yet and I've been laying here watching Colby sleep for what feels like forever. After our shower last night, I shared with him that today I was driving to the city to meet with the crown attorney. He immediately wanted to come with me, both out of fear I might not come back and concern that I shouldn't do it alone. I loved that he was invested and didn't pry for details even though I know he wanted to.

All I could share with him last night was that I always felt my dad wasn't a good person and I didn't know why. It's weird when you can't put your finger on something about someone, especially when it's your own father. My mom died when I was just a kid and I barely remember her, but what I do remember is warm hugs and always feeling safe. As I got older that feeling gradually slipped away until I felt like I was living with a stranger.

My dad provided what I needed. Clothes as I grew and food in the fridge. He even paid my fees for hockey the one year I said I wanted to try it. He never came to the games, but I was allowed to play. There were gifts on birthdays and holidays, but the cold detachment was always there at the fringe of it all. Like he was an actor in his own play.

The older I got, the more the feeling my dad wasn't who he seemed to be grew. As a minor, I knew I was stuck until I could get an education and job and be on my own. But it was a long road of waiting and by the time I was sixteen, I had withdrawn and barely said a word to anyone. My dad didn't seem to care, but now I suspect part of the reason he married Colby's mom was to give me something to care about. Something he could use as leverage over me.

And boy he couldn't have been more right.

Colby shifts against me and squeezes tighter in his sleep. Like he knows what I'm thinking about, and I stroke my hand down his back.

Colby and his mom were what I'd been missing. Hailey was a real mom and she loved me like I truly was her own son. Which made it super awkward when her real son kissed me.

But Colby was more than an attraction. We had a connection. This unexplainable draw to each other that I'd never had before. Not that I had many. I did kiss a guy in the back of the theater once, and while I liked it, there was no spark or fire. Just another pair of lips.

Colby turned everything on inside me. He made me think ahead to the future and believe I could be something. He made me feel wanted and loved and so incredibly desired. Nothing was hotter than having Colby kiss me and tell me he loved me. He made me wish for the dream, for the everything.

My dad knew I was invested with Hailey and Colby. He knew I'd given them my heart and had a renewed sense of purpose with life. I had a goal and the support to achieve it. He didn't care that I was gay. Hell, he knew Colby was already. Colby had already come out to his mom before we even showed up.

But what I didn't know was that my dad had plans for me and when he came to me late that night with emotionless eyes telling me to pack my shit and get in the car, I had no choice but to listen. Because Hailey and Colby didn't deserve to be caught in whatever stupid game he was playing and for five years I've ached to get back and tell them I'm sorry. Five years I've wanted to tell them the story of why I left and never contacted them.

Which is why I'm paying a visit to the crown attorney today.

When your dad is a crooked cop and you have information, you can't be too careful.

Chapter 12

Dante

*O*kay, just walk into the building Dante, you can do this.

A cursory glance at my appearance in a shop window has me doubt how this will all go down. I mean, I look like the quintessential criminal in my faded jeans, worn t-shirt and shoes that no man in his twenties would be caught dead in. Add the eyebrow piercing and the forearm tattoo and I'm not what you call high society in this part of town. I also need a haircut.

With a deep breath, I pull open the doors to the giant office building and step into the climate controlled foyer.

"How can I help you today?"

A lady with a friendly face sits behind a reception desk. A very scary looking guard stands off to the side of her. If there was a contest for the best *don't-even-try-it-with-me-today-or-I-will-hand-you-your-ass-on-a-platter* face, he'd win uncontested. I'm not about to piss him off.

"I uh, have an appointment with Mr. Scott at 11 A.M. Dante Perrish."

I wipe my hands on my pants again. I've not felt this off kilter since I was plunked in a world I didn't know all those years ago by my father and told to figure it out. Like figuring out how to survive in a world of drugs, dirty money, snitches and violence was something anyone could just "figure out." If I survived all that shit, surely this is a walk in the park.

"You can take the elevator to the sixth floor. You'll be greeted there and taken to his office."

Before I move to the elevator the guard motions me to him.

"Arms out to the sides, please."

Ah, it makes sense for them to frisk me before I visit a powerful attorney. I'm sure he has many people who don't want to send him Christmas cards or brake if he's crossing the street.

Once the guard finishes his once over and I get a free ass grab, (thank you surly guard, hope you liked it) he motions me to the elevator and I rush inside to hit the button for the sixth floor. When it opens I'm once again greeted by a smiling woman who takes me to a conference room and offers me coffee, which I decline. Caffeine would not be advisable at this point in time. Not even a little.

And now I wait, which turns out to not be long because Mr. Scott arrives with a quiet knock a few minutes later.

"Dante, it's nice to see you again."

His soft voice outside the courtroom throws me and he extends his hand with a genuine smile.

"Thank you, Mr. Scott. If we were meeting under other circumstances I'd say the same."

With a chuckle he sits across from me.

"That's fair. But honestly, I'm happy to see you well. I did what I could to make sure you were sent somewhere... more friendly."

Even though I was convicted and he knew I was set up, he asked for leniency on the prison I'd be sent to and somehow, it was granted. It's one of the reasons I'm back today. To try to pay back a little of his kindness.

"I'm very grateful for that. Being in prison was a nightmare on its own, but that helped me get through it."

Which is the truth. I was placed with white collar criminals, most who were just stupid and got caught. They were all trying to get through it like I was. I made sure to not make friends, but I remained polite and followed all the rules. I even played the odd game of Scrabble during free time with a few of them, but I never told them anything about me.

Ever.

"I trust your probation officer knows you're here?"

"Yes, I asked first thing and she gave me a card in case I were to be... I don't know, confronted or in trouble or something."

"Good, don't lose it." He leans forward on the table and his face gives nothing away. It's what makes him a damn good lawyer. Probably a great poker player too, because I have zero idea what his thoughts are right now. "How can I help, Dante? And just so you know, this meeting is all off record. Purely conversation."

Swallowing, I know what he means. It's not my first foray into these off the record talks.

"I want to know if it's too late to give you information. Particularly on my father."

He tilts his head. "Why now?"

And this is the hard part. "He used me. Robbed me of five years of my life. He threatened people I love and I was a coward not giving you information the first time. But I... I thought if I could just get through the time and finally see them again, I'd be okay."

I need to pause and blink back the angry tears. I wish I had accepted the coffee now, if only to give me something to focus on instead of the floor.

"But I'm not okay, and now I'm scared. Because what if he tries to do it again? What if he does something worse? What if he ruins someone else's life? I don't think I could live with that." I meet his eyes again. "I want him to get what he deserves."

My words hang in the air as Mr. Scott processes what I've said.

"It's highly unusual for someone to come to me after a trial willing to give up information after the fact. It comes with risk to you, Dante."

"I'm aware of that."

"He could still threaten your family, perhaps worse if he knows you're up to something."

It's a thought that I've given too much headspace to over the past few months, but I can't sit here and do nothing.

"He made his teenage son run drugs for him! He manipulated me, Mr. Scott, in a way that no parent ever should! Because he made a mistake, I had to pay for it and he knew I'd say yes. He knew I'd fucking say yes because I had everything I'd ever wanted at the age of nineteen and he was still a poor excuse for a human." Despite my best efforts to keep them at bay, the warm tears flow down my cheeks. "I hate him. Now that I've confirmed my stepmother and brother are indeed okay, I need him to hurt like I did."

I can't hold the rage in anymore. I never talked at the time of the trial because I was so terrified he'd do something to Colby and Hailey and follow through with his threats to make their life hell. To kick them out on the street, to stop helping pay for Colby's horse upkeep and sell her for dog food. And I knew he'd do it without a single regret just to make me feel guilty. There was no way I'd let Colby suffer through that. My father knew every single button to press to make me do what he needed. And I folded, like he knew I would, because you do anything to protect the people you love.

And I loved Colby more than my own freedom.

"Dante, I understand your frustration and pain. He's not a good man, but you've just gotten in touch with Colby again, and maybe there's other ways."

I see it then. His jaw ticks and I know he's not telling me everything. A small disturbance in his mask. While it's off the record, he can still only reveal so much to me. He's a lawyer after all, and a damn good one.

"Hypothetically, Mr. Scott, if there were other ways to burn my father, would I or my family still be in danger?"

He chews his lower lip as his cool eyes assess me and the silence hangs in the room.

"Possibly, but what I want you to do is go home and think about it. Your stepbrother is planning to do a business expansion, isn't he?"

His statement throws me. How would he know that? Or is this some kind of code I need to pick up on? He nods, ever so slightly a signal to hold off on what to tell him. But why?

"He is, yes. He's meeting with the investor next week."

"Excellent. I'm positive it will work in his favour. Will you at least think about what you want to do until then?"

This couldn't get any more bizarre and not at all how I wanted this meeting to go down. But then again, it feels like it may be working like I hoped anyway.

"Uh, I can. Might as well sleep on it, right?"

He stands to show me out. "Exactly, sometimes things become more clear in the morning or after a visit with family. It was truly nice to see you again, Dante. I know I'll see you again soon."

With those words he leads me to the elevator, says goodbye and my head is spinning even more than when I came in here.

Something's going on and this time, I'm not the one keeping a secret.

Chapter 13

Colby

The bed dips and a warm body presses into mine drawing me out of the fitful sleep I was in.

"Hey, Colbs. Sorry to wake you."

Dante drops a kiss on the back of my neck and his arm around my waist pulls me closer to him. I wiggle my butt back, sighing with the comfort of finally knowing he's home and safe.

"Wha timezit?" I mumble and his lips curve against my skin.

"It's 1 A.M. Go back to sleep."

Lacing my fingers in his, I draw his hand to my mouth, kissing his roughened palm.

"I can't just go back to sleep when you're all up in my business. Besides, I was barely sleeping."

"You were worried about me." Dante's voice is sad. I know he feels guilty that I worry, but I can't help it.

I shift and roll over, letting my eyes adjust to the dark. "I'll always worry about you, so don't be like that. I can't help it and it's not your fault. It's a me issue."

His thumb grazes my cheek and he drops another kiss on my forehead.

"I never want to cause you any more pain, Colbs. Ever. Even worry."

Oh god, just seeing him hurting like this makes my whole body ache. I wish I could carry all his pain for him. For both of us, really.

"Hey, it's okay. You're not hurting me."

Even in the darkness I can read that face. I trace my finger across his brow, smoothing his eyebrows and smiling when my finger runs over the metal bar on his right eyebrow.

"I like this by the way. It suits you. When did you get it?"

He takes my hand and lightly kisses my finger tips. "For my twentieth birthday. I thought it made me fit in better with the people I was around."

"Do you like it?"

He rests his forehead against mine with a sigh. "I no longer hate it. It reminds me that I can adapt when I need to. That I've made it through some hard times and even if I didn't fit in, I made it."

"You did make it," I whisper, bringing my hand to his cheek. "You did what you needed to and you're back where you should be."

His arm around my waist pulls me closer and he drops his head to my shoulder. The shuddering breath and the moisture on my skin has me squeeze my arms around him more. Dante never cried when we were teenagers, ever. Even when Babe stepped on his foot once, breaking his baby toe, he never cried. Whatever happened today upset him, but I know now, he'll tell me when he's ready.

"I love you, you know. Whatever is going on, I'm still going to love you, no matter what."

"I love you so much Colbs, but I can't tell you much yet, but I will. You trust me?"

"With everything I have, D. Everything."

"Let's get some sleep then, I have a llama I need to care for tomorrow and you need to be at work."

He wraps himself around me so tight, it's what I imagine being in a cocoon must feel like. A big, safe, muscley cocoon. And even though I'm not used to sleeping tangled up with another person, I fall asleep to the rhythm of his breath and his heartbeat in my ear.

"Hey Colby, there's a shipment here. I've signed for it. Do you want me to unpack it or leave it for you?"

Shelby, my part-time employee, pokes her head into the office. I've been back here for what feels like an eternity trying to get my head around all my bank statements and loan information. I anticipated a headache from it all and so far I'm right. The dull ache at the back of my head started an hour ago. I took the over the counter meds since I still need to get some work done and so far it's keeping it at bay. I'll take the small win.

"Why don't you go ahead and start with it." I pinch the bridge of my nose. "I think it's mostly restock anyway. Just make sure you check the invoices as you unpack please."

Left alone again, I search the box of my documents and pull out my loan agreement. The legal sized sheets are folded and bent to fit in the box and it's the thickest document in there. It's always easy to find. When I first started searching for loans to purchase a business, even though I was a business major, I was vastly overwhelmed at the amount of capital I had to already have in order to get any kind of funding. Which is really shitty logic. If I had the funds myself I wouldn't be looking for help in the first place.

But I did win a grant from an entrepreneur contest for a few thousand dollars which wouldn't get me far, but it was a start. I kept my part-time job at Tilt-a-Whirl brewery in town doing whatever they needed to ensure I had income. The owners even pointed me in the right direction for suppliers and helped me with my business plan.

My mom offered to cosign a loan, but I was determined to figure it out on my own. My stepdad even offered to help, but I wanted nothing to do with his money or him.

One night I stumbled on an episode of the *Dragon's Den* and angel investing was mentioned, so I looked into it, found a few forums and applied. While I was excited to be chosen and given a loan with decent rates, a few things weren't quite standard with our agreement.

Flipping open the pages, I review the non-standard clauses again like I do every few months. It was requested I send my current profit and loss statements every four months along with any changes I may have made to my business plan. At the time, I didn't think much of it since the investor asked to remain anonymous.

I assumed it was just the investor wanting to keep their fingers in their investment and not much else.

But last week's email requesting a face to face meeting has me on edge. I'm to bring the usual documents with me to the meeting and while it's a five year term loan, I'm just coming up on two years. The investor requested a clause to call the loan if sufficient benchmarks hadn't been met at the two year mark.

Again, I brushed it off at the time because I so badly wanted to get the business started. Now as I stare at the words on the document an unease creeps back in. If they call the loan, I can't pay the balance owing. They also didn't specify what benchmarks. I'd been meeting my own personal goals and I was profitable, but it's not like I have a huge slush fund built up. It's a good business, but it's not good enough to pay off a loan after only two years.

"I'm just over reacting. Maybe they just want to meet me because my numbers are so good. Or maybe they want to offer me hands-on help, which would be cool."

I finish printing out the statements they requested and the update of my business plan. I also include the winning bid of the contractor Dante helped me choose for the renovation and addition of an ice cream bar. Wouldn't hurt to show my thoroughness, right?

While they print from my portable printer, an email notification pops up.

My mom and stepdad are again asking for a good day to visit. Is it bad if I just reply and ask my mom to come alone? And how do I tell them Dante is back? And that gets my mind spinning again as

I re-read the email. The first email came just before Dante showed up. Do they already know he's out and want to tell me? But Dante said his dad was a bad person and he was involved with him going away so that wouldn't make sense.

My headache escalates and I push back all the conspiracy thoughts swirling. This is real life, not some kind of TV drama show.

I don't answer the email either. I'll have to speak to Dante about it first. He's been through enough and I don't want him uncomfortable in his own home if they visit, even though I know he'd love to see my mom.

That thought puts a smile on my face.

My Dante is finally home. With me. And I intend to keep it that way.

Chapter 14

Dante

"Here, Mittens."

I make the kissing sound you would call out for a cat and crouch lower. The llama turns her head from the wall and glares at me. It's a really creepy look.

"Don't be so mad, Mittens. I'm not gonna hurt you. You must be hungry, sweetheart. You haven't eaten."

Since Mittens arrived she's not eaten a thing. If she did it's so miniscule it's not noticeable, and I'm concerned. An idea comes and I leave her to walk across the grounds to Alec's place. I don't know if he's in, but there's a car I don't recognize in front of his place.

He opens the door at my knock and he's not alone. A man with blonde shaggy hair waves over Alec's shoulder as he spritzes water on the spider plant hanging in the living room. Alec bites into the sandwich he's holding and my own stomach growls.

"Hey, Dante. What's up?"

"Uh, I'm not interrupting anything, am I?"

He cocks his head, "No, why?"

"You have company and I —"

He shakes his head. "That's just Zane. He thinks I neglect my plants so he comes over to take care of them." He motions me inside. "But he also brings me sandwiches, so I put up with it."

"Just tell him all you care about is the food, Alec. Honesty is the best policy even though my heart will shatter."

Alec rolls his eyes. "He brought extra, have you eaten yet?"

"No, I haven't actually."

"Could you please eat it and tell me if you like it?" Zane calls as he walks over to another plant and starts misting.

Alec hands me a paper wrapped sandwich with the logo of the local brewery on it. I didn't come here for free lunch but I'll take it and it does sound amazing.

"Zane operates the restaurant at the brewery in town and he's always testing recipes. I'm the guinea pig."

"Don't act like you hate it!" Zane sings and Alec shakes his head with a sigh.

"I don't hate it. Usually."

"Hey!" Zane holds the water bottle and adjusts the nozzle. "Don't make me spray you, Mr. Ranch Foreman."

Okay, so this guy is a tad weird, but he brought a sandwich that looks and smells amazing. He's talking to plants like nobody is listening and Alec stares after him with a look I can't quite place.

Biting into the sandwich, I can't contain the moan that comes out of my mouth. "OMG, what is this, Zane? It's fucking amazing."

"Yes!" He abandons the spray bottle and joins us in the kitchen. "It's slow roasted bison in honey beer BBQ sauce, sauteed red onion and provolone cheese melted on top. Everything is made local except the cheese. It would taste better if you had it fresh, though. Now the bread is soggy, but I'm glad you like it. You should come by the brewery some time."

"Maybe I should. Thanks so much for the sandwich, really. But I came here to see if you had any small bowls, plastic or stainless I could use?"

"How big do you need?" Alec opens his cupboards and pulls out a few sizes and they are all massive.

"Do you have anything small enough for a cat to eat out of?"

He rummages again and finds a smaller tupperware type container. "Is this okay?"

"This could work. Do you mind not getting it back?"

"Uh, no. That's fine. Hey, I'm gonna need you to help me check on the sheep later, too. Dan wants them brought back to the near pasture, there's been some wolf sightings."

"Sure thing. I'm just trying to get Mittens to eat so come find me when you're ready."

I leave them to it and eat my sandwich as I walk back to Mittens. It's seriously an amazing sandwich. Zane said I should eat it when it's fresh and it occurs to me, I've never been on a date with Colby. I've never been able to take him for dinner and look at the stars or kiss him outside his front door.

That time of our life was stolen and rather than lament the loss, I want to make new memories and have them mean so much more because of what we lost, not in spite of it. I always hoped we'd get a second chance and now that it's here, I don't want to waste a single moment of it.

I wish I could tell him the whole story now. It was my intention to, after visiting the attorney. But Mr. Scott's cryptic speaking and warnings hold me back. I don't want to put Colby in harm's way by saying something I shouldn't, and he's being so damn patient. He deserves the answers and he'll get them, but for now it's life as normal.

As normal as life can be when you're trying to convince a llama she's not a cat, that is.

Mittens is still in the corner and I'm beginning to wonder if she's even moved at all in the last three days. Poor thing. Here's hoping my idea might work, at least. Using a jack-knife in the barn, I cut the bowl down so it's more shallow and make sure there's no sharp edges and scoop some corn feed into it.

Crouching low, I shake the bowl and make the kissy noises again. I'm rewarded with a turn of her head and a twitching nose.

"Mittens, you need to eat. I don't want you getting sick, girl."

She continues sniffing the air and I decide to be brave and step into the pen to get the food closer to her. She lets me take one step before humming loud and I've learned that noise is my cue to stay back. So I sit on my butt and place the food dish as far as my arm can stick it between us. And then I wait. Mittens continues to stare at me, but she no longer hums and she keeps twitching her nose and ears. It's definitely progress and I'll take it.

"Hey, Dante!" Alec greets as he enters the barn and Mittens scowls before tucking her head back into the wall. I guess that's it for me today.

"Hey, time to go round up sheep?"

"If you don't mind. How's Mittens?"

Dusting my butt off I exit the pen with a sad backward glance. "It's slow, but I think she's starting to trust me. Or at least tolerate me for now."

Alec claps me on the back with a laugh, "Isn't that always how the best friendships start?"

I park my beat up car behind Colby's little red Honda, happy to be home.

Home.

A place I haven't had for so long, it feels foreign to say it even in my head.

I stayed far later than usual helping Alec herd the sheep, and sadly we found one dead, most likely from the wolf he spoke about. But Dan can't afford to lose any of the flock, it's one of his biggest income streams and the only animals on the ranch that aren't rescues.

Letting myself into the apartment, I quietly move about the dark space and wonder if Colby is even home. Landon's truck is missing so he could be out with him. I enter his bedroom and before I can flick on the lamp his voice stops me.

"I'm here."

"It's only 9 P.M., is it your head?" I shuffle to the bed and ease onto the edge.

"Fucking financial statements and bank statements and I hate numbers." He laughs softly and reaches a hand for me. "God, I hate numbers."

"I remember." Colby was good at basic math and he was smart enough to understand how markups and profit worked, but he hated all the spreadsheets and analysis. He always had. Math to him was just a torture and I often helped him with math homework. It was an excuse to spend time with him at first, but it worked in my favour eventually.

"I'm going to take a shower, do you need anything before I do?"

Squeezing my hand he drops words to make my heart burst, "Just you, so don't take too long."

I squeeze his hand back, "I'll be two shakes of a lamb's tail."

Colby's snort laugh is a sound I've missed. "You've been on the ranch too long. Get into the shower already. A lamb's tail... " He trails off in soft laughter and I'm just happy I'm the cause of it.

Moving around the dim room, I leave my dirty clothes in a pile and wrap a towel around my waist to dart across to the bathroom. When the man you think of twenty-four seven tells you to hurry, you listen.

I think I set speed records for shower time and rush to dry myself off. My reflection in the mirror is no longer a fresh teenager full of hope. It's all in my eyes for anyone to see. The sparkle of hope faded years ago, replaced with a determination that both disappoints me and drives me.

What does Colby think of this new me?

He likes my eyebrow piercing, but he hasn't commented on much else. I know he loves me, he's said so. But he's not asked me anything other than what I can't yet tell him. Running my fingers along my arm tattoo, I smile at the hidden part of it that's just for him. He definitely hasn't had time to notice that yet.

Shaking my head, I finish drying and wrap the towel around my waist before hurrying back to the bedroom. When I enter, Colby has the lamp on and he's scrolling through his phone with a frown. When he sees me the smile he beams my way makes my heart clunk out of beat.

"That was fast. Did you miss me that much?"

I let the towel drop to the floor and his gaze burns a path along my body.

"I've got a lot of days missing you banked. So, yeah, I did."

He flips the covers back and invites me to slide next to him, which I do and always will. I don't think Colby knows how much I'd do for him if he asked me.

He slides his leg in between mine, laying his head on my shoulder. His fingers dance across my stomach and chest in a rhythmic pattern as he squeezes me closer.

"What's on your mind, Colbs?" Some things change so much you can barely recognize what they once were, but Colby trailing patterns over my flesh when he's got something on his mind is a nervous habit I'll never forget.

His warm breath caresses my skin. "You always knew when I had something on my mind." He places a soft kiss on my chest. "I don't even know where to start."

"Just start at the beginning, that's easiest."

He swirls his fingers in the hair on my chest and I chuckle. "Are you enraptured by my chest hair?"

"You didn't have this before!" There's a pause as his voice lowers, "I like it. I've missed so much of you."

I smooth my hand on his back in the old pattern I know keeps him grounded and feeling safe. Muscle memory might be involved, but so are the memories of calming him when he needed it.

My voice is gravel filled, "We've missed a lot of each other and I'm sorry for that. But we have the rest of our lives to make up for it."

"We do."

The silence is comfortable, both of us content to hold each other, but there's something on his mind he has yet to say. My fingers travel to his hair and I run my hands through the soft waves and kiss the top of his head. His hair smells like the shampoo I just used, strawberry mint. While it's perfect for Colby, sweet and soft just like him, I'll have to find one of my own.

His hand reaches across to pull my tattooed forearm to him and his fingers trace the lines of the tattoo. It's a forest scene, evergreen trees in various heights and they circle my arm from wrist to elbow. On the inside of my wrist, one of the tree trunks is different, rounded like his favourite candy and the tree has a swirled design in the branches while the others don't.

"Why did you get a tattoo? I don't remember you ever saying you wanted one."

"I didn't, but again, it was to fit in. Even though I didn't want to fit in, I tried to not stand out, and I was the only one in the crowd without any tattoos." I turn my arm so he can examine the inside trees and his fingers pause over the swirled design there.

He raises his head and comes closer while still tracing the design.

"Is this... is this what I think it is?"

His voice wavers as he examines the horse hidden in the tree. A horse very much like Babe. While I didn't want a tattoo, it did provide me comfort some nights when I was in my cell and missing him more than anything. If I laid my wrist over my heart in those dark hours, I'd imagine Colby receiving a silent message and know I was thinking of him. The tattoo artist was decent too, considering he was a guy also involved with laundering the drug money of the circle I was with. Not that his skill was affected by the operation, but sometimes you lose passion for your work if you do it for the wrong reasons.

I point to the tree trunk. "It is, and this is your favourite candy." The trunk is a Lik-a-Stix from his favourite Fun Dip candy. But it's all artfully blended into the whole tattoo. "Babe and your candy are there so I could feel like you were a part of me anytime. The rest of the trees are there because I like nature and I loved it when we'd hike those paths at the rec area. It was like our own world where nobody could touch us." His eyes shine and I shake my head. "Don't cry Colby. It's not your fault."

"I hate you had to go through all this, D. I fucking hate it."

I cup my palm to his cheek and he leans into my touch. "I know, and I hate seeing you so down over something you had no control over."

"But I pushed you away when you came back. I didn't give you a chance to explain. I wanted to know everything and I didn't even know you were living in your car." He swallows hard and I wish he wouldn't be so hard on himself. He had every right to push me away. "I hate that I even doubted you. Ever."

"Colby, you're human, so stop. I have no hard feelings."

He places a kiss on the horse in the tattoo. "You know what I did? To keep you close to me?"

My heart resumes its off beat rhythm again. "What?"

Untangling himself from me, he walks over to his closet and I smile at his horseshoe print boxers. He returns with a square red box and sits on the edge of the bed, forcing me to wiggle back and give him room.

"When I went away to college, it was hard for lots of reasons, but mostly because you'd only been gone for a few months and I still hadn't accepted you might actually be gone." He smooths a shaking hand over the lid. "I went into your room and took some of your things to keep with me." He laughs softly and wipes at his eyes. "I slept with one of your t-shirts on my pillow for months."

I swallow back the rush of emotion for Colby. It's hard not to hate myself seeing him relive his pain. I wanted so badly to protect him and make sure his life was free of all the sadness and obstacles. Instead it feels like maybe I was a coward for leaving, because he's not as happy as I wanted him to be.

Lifting the lid, he holds various items he found in my room and tells me why he kept them. With each one, my heart breaks more.

"I saved your deodorant, it smelled like you and I didn't want to forget it. Two t-shirts, this one because it was your favourite and this one because it was thrown on your bed and not in the laundry, so I knew you had worn it and... god, I'm such a loser."

"No, you're not. You were trying to keep a memory alive. I'm honoured and I feel sick knowing you felt like this all this time."

I push myself up to sit and cover his hand with mine. "I'm so grateful you loved me enough to do this, but I'm so fucking sorry it happened, Colby."

He rubs at his temple and I know he needs to rest or he'll be in so much pain tomorrow.

"Let's get some rest, baby."

He places the lid on the box and slips under the covers with me again. I flick off the lamp and massage his head as he clings to me like an octopus.

This meeting with his investor has to happen soon. My father needs to pay for putting Colby through this, I've already paid enough.

Chapter 15

Colby

When I woke up alone this morning, I wished Dante didn't have such an early start. He'd left me a note and the simple domesticity of it made my heart skitter all over.

Good morning Colbs,

I didn't want to leave you sleeping, but work is a necessity (they didn't warn us work could be early!)

Anyway, I know this is a huge thing to ask, but now that I have an address (YAY!) could you go to the insurance place downtown for me and finish the application for my car insurance? Talk to a lady named Carol, she has everything waiting to go but since I'm at the ranch all the time I keep missing her, and you know I shouldn't be driving without it.

That's what the cash is for, she already quoted me. Hope I see you later today and maybe the boss will let me take a ride with you.

Love,

Dante

I'm still holding the note with hearts in my eyes when Landon disturbs my fuzzy moment.

"Hey roomie! Is there coffee left?"

Freshly showered and smiling like always, he peers into the coffee pot.

"I think so. Go ahead and take it, I'll make fresh stuff if you're in a hurry."

He reaches for a mug and drains the pot Dante must have made. Landon scans my bed head and my sleep pants.

"No work for you today?"

I shake my head. "No, I had Shelby scheduled so I could prepare for this investor thing." I hold the note and money up. "But Dante asked if I could do a favour for him and now I think I might avoid the paperwork altogether and go for a ride instead."

He peers over the edge of the canary yellow mug with, *Don't worry, be happy* on it. It's Landon's life motto.

"Things are working out well then? I must say, I'm impressed with his work ethic, not to mention how happy you look right now."

There's no way to hold back my happiness over having Dante here. I can't say it's a perma grin, but it's close.

"He works hard and... he's just trying to make up for shit. He's a good guy, no – the best guy and I'm really happy he came back."

"I sense a 'but' coming."

Landon sips his coffee and I move behind him to make one of my own.

"No, not a but. It's just a bumpy road to fix a lot of things that were broken that were neither of our faults. But he carries all the blame. I know he's devastated that I took it so hard, but so did he. God, Lan, you know the tattoo on his arm?"

"I've seen it, a bunch of trees?"

"It's trees, yes, but those trees remind him of our hikes together." I comb a hand through my hair, "And on the inside of his arm, hidden in one of the trees is a design of Babe and a Fun Dip stick." Of all the things to remember, that Fun Dip stick keeps coming back. It's ridiculously sweet, both the sentiment and the candy.

Landon tilts his head. "He's romantic, is he?"

Sighing like a schoolgirl, I admit it. "He is and I love it, but it hurts to know he hurts. I'm struggling with that. I don't know why he disappeared yet, either. I just know it's something to do with Brian and he'll tell me soon."

Landon curls his lip. "I don't like that guy."

"Me neither. Last night Dante asked what was on my mind, but I didn't tell him because he was already so sad. I know Brian did something bad and I'm really worried about mom. What if she's in danger? What if he's putting her in danger? Dante loves her too, and he might already be thinking the same thing as me." I lean against the counter, fidgeting with the sugar bowl. "Mom has been emailing me for a visit and I've put it off because she said it's both of them coming. I don't know why, but it feels off."

"You think they're coming because they know Dante is here?"

"No, actually. The first email came before he even showed up. Unless they knew he was coming and wanted to talk to me. But if so, why not just call me?"

Landon finishes his coffee and places the mug in the dishwasher. "Good question. Maybe you should call her instead? Find out what's going on?"

"I probably should, but I want this meeting out of the way first. It's causing me way more stress than needed and while mom is concerning, the store takes precedence right now. I can only deal with one major occurrence at a time."

Landon agrees for me to focus on squaring away my loan meeting and store first. He leaves for work with a wish for me to have a stress free day and enjoy myself. Thinking that sounds like great advice, I get dressed for the ranch and leave the house to run Dante's errand before I enjoy the rest of my day.

Whatever my mom and Brian want to see me for can wait a little longer.

Grabbing the bag with what I hope is a surprise late afternoon picnic lunch from the back seat, I slap my cowboy hat on my head and first walk to the barn where Dante said he'd be with Mittens. The barn door is propped open and I poke my head around the corner slowly. Dante mentioned Mittens was still skittish and not eating. He hopes to get close enough to hand feed her and just in case he's close to that point, I don't want to disturb.

His voice, sweet and encouraging, lilts through the stale air of the barn.

"It's okay, sweetie. I'm not going to hurt you. I'm just here to help and you need to eat."

Dante is next to the llama and she's allowing him to stroke her fur which is a huge win for him! I stay back and watch, hoping she finally takes some food from him.

He first holds up the small bowl of corn feed and she does sniff at it but won't eat, instead choosing to pull back again and Dante's shoulders sag. Mine slump along with him, he wants so badly for this llama to eat and come out of its shell.

"I'm going to leave the dish right here, okay? Maybe you want to eat in private? Are you a loud chewer and you're nervous maybe?" I grin listening to his words. "Or maybe you're going to spill? It's not like it's spaghetti on your white fur. And it's just me, so if that's your worry, Mittens, just know I'm messy too." He pushes up to standing and Mittens still hasn't touched her food, but she's actively listening to him if her ear twitches mean anything.

He reaches over to pet her ears again and she turns her head back to the wall.

"It's okay, I get it. I'm not giving up on you, okay? If Colby won't give up on me I sure as heck won't give up on you."

I duck back and take a few steps away from the barn to draw a breath. Dante's right though. I won't give up on him. Quite the opposite, in fact. I want us to talk about our future. My morning has been full of thinking about us and the conversations we still need to have.

Dante steps out of the barn then, pulling his hat down against the afternoon sun. When he notices me, his eyes light up and it's possibly the best sight in the modern living world.

"Hey, you. You came."

He kisses my lips with a tender touch and caresses the top of my cowboy hat. "You always did look great with this on your head and a horse between your thighs."

"I didn't know you had such a cowboy fetish. Should I be concerned with you working here? Surrounded by other men in cowboy hats and horses?" I tease.

"Nah, it's just you, Colbs. Only ever been you."

I duck my head with a grin, overcome by his sweetness. "Is Dan gonna let you take a ride and knock off early?"

The man in question shouts Dante's name from the far side of the yard while waving. Dante laces his fingers in mine. "I haven't actually asked yet, let's find out." With a tug he pulls me by his side as we walk towards Dan.

"Hi ya, Colby! How's things? Are you here for a ride?" Dan asks. His always present smile in place

"It's good!" I smile over at Dante. "It's great now that I have this guy back."

Dan's gaze softens. "I'm glad you two worked it out. I've never seen you take off and ride like that, I was worried."

Hanging my head, I try to apologize again, but Dante speaks for me. "You know it was my fault and I was worried too. Thanks for going after him and making sure he and Babe were okay. I owe you so much for that."

Dan chuckles as he looks between the two of us. "Funny you should say that. I have a favour to ask and I think you'll both be okay with it."

"Well, if it's work related I don't think I can say no, can I?" Dante jokes and I wonder what the heck has Dan smiling at us like this.

Dan claps his hands together in front of him. "Okay, the new horse, Charlie? He likes Babe. I'd appreciate it if you could take him on a trail ride and make sure he's okay with the saddle and tell me how he does before I allow others to ride him."

"Since I'm here to take Babe out and I brought us food, does this mean I can ask him to come with me and he's not really working?" I grin at Dan and hold up the bag of snacks I picked up at Wild Baloney before coming here. "Because I wanted to take him on a sort of date."

"Well aren't you a sweetheart," Dan teases with a smile. "Yes, he's off the clock. Take Charlie and use the dark saddle with the blanket on top. Tell me how he does when you get back."

"You heard the man, let's go for a ride!" Laughing, Dante pulls me after him to the pasture to call the horses over. As the horses figure out we're the bringers of snacks and draw closer to us, Dante steals my hat and places a lingering kiss on my lips. "Time to ride, Colbs. It's time to ride."

The smile hasn't left my face since we started our ride. Dante had only just begun learning how to ride Babe when he left. She's such an easy going horse, she's perfect for beginners. I insisted for him to ride her while I rode the new horse, since I had more experience. In case Charlie spooked or bucked, I wanted to be riding him so Dante didn't get himself hurt.

I still had my best horse on a ride and I was with the man who stole my heart. The two loves of my life in a gorgeous setting with a somewhat romantic picnic planned. I'd been wishing for this very scene for five years.

When the trail widened I pulled my horse up next to Dante. "How's the ride going? Is your ass sore yet?" I snicker as he adjusts in the saddle with that tell tale shift of someone new to the experience.

"You wouldn't be teasing me so much if I said that to you in the bedroom."

His words, delivered so smoothly, catch me off guard and if I wasn't already holding onto the saddle horn I just may have fallen off.

"Ah, about that," I manage to squeak, and Dante laughs full and deep. It's music to my ears and I reach over to touch his arm.

"There's a gorgeous clearing up ahead. The horses can drink from a stream and we can tether them in the field while we sit."

"Is that code for something more fun?" He wiggles his eyebrows and pulls a bark of laughter from me.

"Fun? You don't think being with me in a field is fun on its own?" I tease.

"It is, but it'd be more fun if when you said sit you really meant make out or blow jobs or something."

I try to sputter a response to his cheeky attitude but he winks and coaxes Babe into a trot, then a gallop and races ahead of me into the meadow before I can form any words. Shaking my head I hold Charlie back as I try to gather the thoughts in my head. I had a big talk planned out before I got to the farm and his comments are part of the conversation we need to have.

When I enter the meadow, he's already dismounted and has led Babe to the stream. He's stretching out next to her and for a moment it's like a dream. I never thought I'd have the two of them together again. He turns when he hears me approach and beams a smile so bright my heart melts.

"You were right, it's gorgeous here."

"It's one of my favourite places."

After the horses drink, we tie them. Normally Babe just roams, but I don't know Charlie well enough for that. I unbuckle the blanket and snacks from the saddle and I make a show of finding a place to spread out the blanket before lowering myself down.

I pat the spot next to me after I sit. "Come sit with me. I have food."

"You don't have to bribe me with food." He laughs.

Dante sits beside me and together we pick at the fruit and cheese and watch the horses graze. The banging of a woodpecker sounds nearby and a few squirrels chatter as they climb the trees, unhappy to have anyone in their space. It's the most peace I've felt in a very long time. When I turn my head to find Dante staring at me, I quickly look away. The butterflies in my gut are mounting a war to fly out.

"So, I got your note and I went to the insurance place for you. I have a temporary slip in my car."

"Thank you."

His voice is quiet and I sneak a look over. Now he drops his head and looks away. It's like we're awkward teenagers all over again when we stumbled our way through that first kiss. And why not make a new first kiss? Sure it's all backwards, but I think it's right.

"So, ah, while I was in town I got you something." I reach into the bag I brought the food in and pull out a small black flip phone. "I don't like not being able to reach you. When you went to the city I just about died waiting and wondering if you were okay. I know money is tight for you so don't worry about it. It's a gift for me too." I laugh nervously and pass him the cell phone. "I added you to my plan and it's just basic phone service. I didn't know if you wanted data, but I can add that too and share with you. But I just... I need to be able to talk to you sometimes and know where you are."

I gulp as Dante wordlessly stares down at the cell in his hand.

"If you don't like that model, there's a few others we could check out if you prefer." I fidget with the lid of the takeout container and

COLBY   133

forge on. "I already gave you a key and we'll give you space in the dresser tonight because you can't just keep piling clothes on the floor. And... we should, um... talk about the butt stuff, er, the—"

He holds up a hand and I press my lips together.

"I'm gonna stop you right there even though it's adorable listening to you babble and demand me to move in with you."

"I wasn't —"

"Colby, stop. Thank you for being so thoughtful to get me a phone. You picked it, so I love it. I'd love to have my own drawer in the dresser. So again, thank you. Now for the other butt stuff," he air quotes my words with a smile, "as you so eloquently put it, yes, lets talk."

I feel the heat in my cheeks. "Sorry, I'm really nervous. It's been a long time since I've talked to anyone about sex, I sort of lost my mind there."

A squirrel trills in agreement as a yellow butterfly floats past. I wish I felt as serene as that butterfly right now. Unfortunately the squirrel racing to and fro is more indicative of what's going on in my head.

"It's an uncomfortable conversation but I'll tell you straight up. I've never been with anyone. Not even a blow job. Never. Only whatever we did together is what I've done. And I know you're wondering, but my prison wasn't like that. There was no nasty stuff happening. And for the two years before that, I never wanted to be with anyone. So when I say it's only been you, it really has."

He waited for me!?

"Oh."

My chest feels tight. He's only ever been with me. I mean, he mentioned it but I didn't think he meant he'd not so much as kissed someone else.

Holy crap.

I clear the clog from my throat. "Ah, I was only with two people. One during college and another about a year ago. Nobody else. So um, I'm not sure what I like and for some reason I guess I figured you'd be experienced or something? Gah, now I sound like I'm calling you a slut. But, ah, my doc said I should have a test anyway and it's good. Well, the results, not the test itself and —"

"Colby."

Dante moves everything out of the way and crawls over to straddle my lap.

"I'm yours. You're mine. I'm basically a virgin, you're not. I love you so much I can't even consider being with anyone else. We'll figure out how we fit together as we go." He cradles my face with his rough hands and kisses me softly on the lips. I open for him, clutching his hips to anchor him to me. He rocks forward, bringing our denim covered groins together and my breath hitches. "Are you okay with that plan?" he mumbles against my lips.

"Yep. Mmhmm, I'm very okay with that."

He abruptly removes himself from my lap and starts packing up our things, leaving me with emotional whiplash.

"Are you in a hurry?"

"Yes. The sooner we get on the horses, the sooner I'll be too uncomfortable to get a hard on. The sooner we're home, the sooner I can be with you." He flashes a sly grin. "And the sooner we can figure things out."

I watch him smashing everything in the bag with a big stupid grin on my face.

"I thought you were hoping to make out in a meadow?"

He waves a hand in the air. "Pfft, I mean yeah, but... let's just get home so we don't have squirrels watching. Those things are creepy."

Laughing at his absurdity, I help him pack our things.

I'm so glad I ditched work today.

Chapter 16

Dante

Is it possible to clench a steering wheel too hard?

Because I think I'm losing feeling in my fingers from the iron grip I have on the thing.

After we packed up and rode the horses down the trail, we ran as fast as they would go across the fields, both of us far too eager to get home and finally come together.

No pun intended.

As teenagers, Colby and I had grand romantic fantasies. Neither of us wanted to do a quick and dirty in the barn. We wanted to be able to spend a night together and truly get to know each other in a way tender lovers would the first time. It was the cheesiest, yet most heartfelt sentiment we'd ever shared, next to saying I love you.

And I waited a long time. We both did. Just because Colby did what any normal twenty-something guy would and was with other people doesn't make it mean anything less.

While we relieved the testosterone rushes with mutual hand jobs and blow jobs, it wasn't what we both craved. We had even planned the overdone lose-the-virginity-night-of-graduation schtick. We planned on booking a room at the cheap Motel 6 where they didn't ask for ID and preferred straight cash. It wasn't the best location but we'd get to share a bed. That was what we both wanted.

I, of course, didn't know that would get ripped away and I certainly didn't expect Colby to remain chaste all these years. Part of me wished he had, but either way it's still our first time together and it means more to me than anything else to give myself to Colby that way. He's always been the one to have my heart, and call me a sentimental fool, but I still wanted to save myself for the one I want to be with forever.

And it was still Colby.

My eyes remained glued on the tail lights of his car the whole drive back. Even though I knew where we were going, I didn't want to lose any kind of visual connection with this man. The last five years put me through hell, physically, mentally and emotionally. Being with Colby, hell finding Colby and hoping he let me back in without knowing the whole story was the most painful roller coaster I'd ever been on. I don't want to take that ride again.

Finally home, our cars turn into the driveway with a crunching of gravel and I release the steering wheel from my death grip.

Home.

God I can't get used to that yet. Colby takes his usual parking space and I tuck my car in behind him. My hands shake so much I need to practice calm breathing techniques I learned in prison before I vibrate out of my skin.

Deep breath in through the nose and sigh it out.

When I open my eyes, Colby has his hip propped on his car in front of me, head cocked just a little to the left as he examines me through the windshield. He holds his cowboy hat over his chest and his fingers slide back and forth over the brim.

His lips tilt slightly, *you okay?,* is what he's asking. In reply I unfold my full six foot frame out of my shitty car and will my knees to keep me standing.

"Hey." I'm the poster boy for smooth and suave conversation starters..

Colby grins back.

"Hey, yourself." He frowns when he notices the shake still in my hand and reaches forward to take my hand in his. "What's wrong?"

"I'm just really nervous. Like, it's all a dream and you'll be gone again."

He threads his fingers in mine, pulling me close to kiss me. His lips brush over mine, a whisper of promise in the late spring air.

"It's just you and me, D. No need to be nervous. I'm not going anywhere."

I nod as we climb the steps of the porch and I grip his hand harder. Before he can unlock the front door, I stop him.

"Wait. Was today our first real date?"

He smiles in the waning daylight. "I think it was. That was my plan when I went out to the ranch today. To see if I could surprise you and take you on a ride, like a date, if Dan wouldn't mind."

"Well if it was a date, I've always wanted to do something after a date. With you, I mean."

He smiles and his blue eyes are brighter than the moon on a clear night. "And what's that?"

I lean in, cupping his cheek in my palm. "I always wanted to kiss you goodnight at the door."

"You were always a gentleman," he whispers before my lips brush over his. Softly at first, we kiss. Those shy tentative kisses that really have no place between us. Not with all we've done and been through. Yet we still fall back to these fumbling moments and find each other all over again. His hat drops to the porch as he brings his hands to my waist and pulls me closer.

"This was just supposed to be a gentle kiss on the porch to say goodnight," I mumble as I trail kisses along his jaw to his neck.

"Oh? Maybe I always wanted to make out on the front porch and hope someone saw me kissing the hot guy in school." He tilts his head so I can kiss his neck. Then I do it again because he gasped a little and I like that sound.

"You thought I was the hottest guy in school?"

"Of course I did." He pulls back and stares into my eyes. "I still do."

And just like that I'm again transported back to when we first explored the attraction between us. Colby just got me. He accepted my quirks and quarks then and he accepts me now, even though he's still in the dark. Those blue eyes I could get lost in forever see me like no one else does. Just like the first time, I swallow hard and whisper, "I think you're the best person I've ever met and I want to kiss you forever."

His eyes register first shock, and then soften when he remembers the words I said to him after we first kissed, too. "God, Dante. You're the most romantic sentimental guy I've ever met. I remember that night. I remember everything."

I brush my nose across his and kiss his lips. "Still true. For the record."

Instead of turning the key in the door and taking it inside, we lose ourselves in each other. Kissing and touching and never pulling away until he has me backed against the porch railing and our breath has turned to needy pants of desire. We only break apart, somewhat reluctantly, when headlights from a vehicle turning into the driveway wash over us in the darkened porch area.

"Must be Landon. Let's go inside," Colby whispers against my ear.

He bends to pick up his hat and turns to open the door, but a familiar voice sounds out.

"Dante? Colby?"

No. Way.

My entire body turns to stone.

Colby takes a protective step in front of me and I don't miss the shocked look on his face.

"Mom? What are you doing here?"

She hesitates and steps forward. "You weren't answering the emails and I tried to call you today but you didn't pick up." She comes closer and Colby blindly reaches back for my hand. When he finds it he squeezes for a show of support.

"Is that really Dante?"

The waver in her voice finally draws a reaction from me. The only woman I ever got to experience motherly love from is in front of me after five years and my body cries out for a hug. But Colby squeezes my hand when I try to move from behind him.

"It's him, Mom. Did you know where he was all this time?"

The long beat of silence has my heart drop to the floor.

"Boys, we need to talk. Please."

Chapter 17

Colby

My mom sits on the couch fiddling with her teacup. It's the most awkward cup of tea I've ever made.

When I said I wanted to be seen making out with the hottest guy in school, I didn't mean it to be my mother who saw us.

Since she showed up and dumped a bucket of cold water on tonight's plans with Dante she's been quiet. And I love my mother, but it's starting to piss me off. Dante hasn't said a word either and I know he's all kinds of mixed up right now. I feel like I'm caught in the middle of this whole card game, except I can't play because someone forgot to deal me in.

Which means my patience is wearing thin for being left out.

"Mom, you wanted to talk and I assumed you meant tonight. So I'd appreciate it if you could at least, you know, talk."

She sets the teacup down. It's one of my favourite cups. Instead of roses or some other delicate floral pattern, it has bright yellow goldfinches on it. I think the scene belongs in a painting and not a teacup.

"I wasn't expecting to see both of you together."

I bristle with her words. "And what does that mean exactly, Mom? Because you didn't answer my question earlier about if you knew where he was this whole time!"

Mom gasps and Dante snaps his head in my direction. I never lose my temper. I'm calm and patient. There's never a time when I feel I need to raise my voice. Even when it's Landon leaving his shoes in the doorway again and I trip over them, spilling my coffee. Not even when Babe gets too frisky and bites me too hard.

I. Never. Yell.

But I'm a cauldron boiling over right now and I need someone to talk. And it needs to be now.

"I didn't know where he was the whole time, no." Mom looks at Dante as she speaks. "I only found out last year where you were, Sweetie. I didn't know." Her tears flow as she speaks her story and I sink to the couch next to her.

She's known for a year?

She releases a shuddering breath and Dante still sits ramrod straight in his chair.

"I overheard Brian talking on the phone one night. He didn't know I was home. With the information I overheard, I knew it was something I had to be careful with."

"How careful, mom? What's going on?"

She turns back to Dante. "Sweetheart, I had no idea what your dad was into. You have to believe me. If I had... "

She takes a moment and inhales several times with her eyes closed. Something I've seen Dante do a thousand times when we were in high school and even earlier tonight. "I knew you two were together, okay? It was plain as day how head over heels you were for each other. So don't be ashamed about that. I know you were hiding from us and you thought there might be small town gossip to hurt us, but I only cared that my boys were happy." She wipes at her eyes. "Because you're both my boys. Dante, you're not my son by blood, but I love you like one. I always have. I think I loved you before I knew I loved your dad."

Dante never cries. Other than the hugs he'd give Mom and the professions of love to me, he was never overly emotional. Ever. But years away from the ones you love and living the hell he must have experienced, that changes a person. It's the first time I've seen any kind of crack in his outward show of emotions to anyone but me.

But my six foot wall of tattooed muscle just broke. A sob slips out and with tears on his face he's in front of my mom, pulling her tiny five foot nothing frame into his arms and crushing her to his chest.

"Hailey, I'm so sorry you and Colby got dragged into this. I'm so fucking sorry."

One of the things I loved when we were kids, is how everything felt right with the three of us. Mom always treated family events like we were all from the same cloth. She never made Dante feel different. Her birthday cards to him were signed *love mom* and she introduced us both as her sons. That part got awkward for me after we kissed, but Mom never stopped treating Dante like he was one of her own.

If I hadn't been in love with Dante, I would've loved him like a brother. We all just fit like perfect puzzle pieces, but whenever

Brian joined us, Dante would withdraw. He wouldn't talk as much and would often excuse himself from the activity. Brian never seemed to care or say anything when Dante would leave. But Mom always noticed.

He finally releases her and she sits back down, finding the tissue box I placed on the table and wiping her eyes. I can't bear to see him so upset. I force myself onto his lap and wrap my arms around him.

"You, okay?" I whisper next to his ear.

He nods and drops a kiss to my forehead.

I smoosh myself next to him on the recliner. "I still don't know what's going on. I promised Dante he could tell me later and now you're here, Mom, telling me you knew something for the last year. You knew I've been hurting since he left and hoping he'd come back. Why didn't you tell me?"

I can't help the accusation that sneaks into my tone. But damn it, she should have told me.

"I had to do a lot of sneaking around and finding the right people to contact before I could even breathe a word of this to you, Colby. Please understand I wasn't trying to hide it from you."

"I'm sorry, Mom. I'm just... this whole thing is stressful and I'm sorry. But you're here now, so fill me in."

She takes a moment to gather her thoughts and I check in with Dante. His squeeze of my hand lets me know he's just as stressed as I am.

"It was last May, Mother's Day weekend. You sent me such a nice card and a beautiful bouquet. I made a comment to Brian that I wished both of my sons could be here." She pauses and takes a sip from the tea that has to be stone cold by now. "Then he said he was sorry Dante fucked up his life and took off and that wasn't a possibility for me. It was the first time he alluded to knowing anything about Dante so I pretended I didn't pick up on it. But it was the way he said it that chilled my blood. Something wasn't right. We had dinner together and I said I was going to take a walk in the park."

Dante's arm tightens around me and his jaw is clenched so tight I'm concerned he'll break his own teeth.

"He must have thought I went out the back door already and he was on the phone. I don't know who he was talking to, but it wasn't good. Whoever it was, he told them, 'find out when the boy is set to be released.' Then he had this horrible laugh I've never, ever heard from him and he said, 'who knew having a son would come in this handy.'"

Dante's chest heaves and I feel sick. He used his son and laughed about it. This sweet, kind human who has my horse tattooed on his arm and saves his Fun Dip stick for me deserves more than that.

"I've spent the last year going behind his back to find out what happened. I'm still not sure, but I have my suspicions." Mom meets Dante's eyes with a silent message I can't decipher.

Dante nudges me to get up and he stands with me. "I just need a few minutes alone." He disappears down the hall and the click of my bedroom door sounds. God, my body screams at me to follow, to not let him be alone anymore.

COLBY   147

"Colby, I wanted to tell you. I wanted you to help me! But if you would've heard the way he said it... " Her voice breaks. "It was so cold and it wasn't him. It wasn't the man I married."

I recall Dante's words and how he always felt like his Dad was detached. Like he was merely there because he had no other choice. He took care of basic needs but nothing more.

"But he was the same guy, Mom. He just hid it. Dante mentioned he always felt like his Dad didn't care."

She sighs, dropping her head into her hands.

"He hasn't told you what happened yet has he?"

"No, he said he needed to take time and he would tell me once I had my investor appointment this week."

Mom lifts her head, sad eyes finding mine. "That's another reason I came. I need to talk to you about that."

The opening of the bedroom door draws our attention back to Dante. Fuck, how can such a giant man look so damn small? I go to him and slip my arms around his waist. "What can I do?"

"Nothing you aren't already doing, Colbs." He motions for me to sit next to mom and he sits on the coffee table in front of us. Clasping his hands he rests his arms on his knees.

He looks between Mom and I and it's in that moment my simmering rage for a man who married my mother turns into a murderous one. Dante has never looked so fragile and broken.

"The last night I was with you Colby, remember I was worried he saw us together and I was concerned he might say something about it or fight with us."

"I remember."

No way I'd ever forget that night.

"I hadn't fallen asleep yet and he came to my room. Just opened the door and walked right in. It was almost 2 A.M. and he was dressed to go. It was like he was ready to work but without his uniform on." He swallows and drops his eyes. "He said... he said to pack what I wanted and get dressed. It was actually a duffel bag he tossed at me. I started to ask why and what was going on. I thought maybe something had happened to Hailey."

Dante's hands shake and both Mom and I reach out to hold him. He shakes us both off and starts pacing the living room with his hands tangled in his hair.

"He told me to shut the fuck the up, because he finally had a use for me and it was just in time. I was ready to fight him and I wasn't going to do a single thing he said. But he knew what it would take to make me do what he wanted. He knew exactly where my weakness was and he fucking used it like the bastard he is." Dante sucks in a breath. "He said if I didn't do as he said and go with him right now, he'd make both your lives hell and I'd never see you again."

My mom gasps as Dante pauses and looks our way. "That's right, Hailey. He was going to go out of his way to hurt you both. He'd obviously been thinking of it, too." He holds up his hand, ticking off each horrible thing as it leaves his mouth. "He said he'd sell Babe out from under Colby and make sure it was to a slaughter house. He wouldn't help with anything for college. He said he'd use his connections to make sure Colby had nothing easy when he did go. He even hinted at knowing some men who didn't care for gays and did bad things." Dante shakes his head, the fury in his eyes burning like a fireball. "He also said to not underestimate him and he would have you fired, Hailey. Then he'd just walk away from you both and let you struggle. He had a whole damn plan, and it was all based on how to make the both of you suffer if I didn't do what he said. And that was just part of his threats."

Dante finally slumps in the chair. "I'm sorry. I thought I was doing the right thing. I was just a scared kid. I thought I was protecting you both. All I ever wanted was a family like anyone else. A place to feel loved and wanted. A group of people to make me feel like I could accomplish anything. I finally had it and he took it away for his own selfish reasons."

"D, what did you have to do for him?" I whisper.

He chews his lip and I know that face. No way will I ever think less of him for trying to protect us, no matter what he did.

My mom speaks up. "He forced you to deliver drugs, didn't he?"

Dante nods his head as my jaw hits the floor. "He drove me two hours away and left me at a warehouse with some guy. I was in a haze for the next two days as all these people explained the process and how to avoid being caught and who the guys were you had to watch out for." His voice is thick as he forces the words out. "I was so scared I just did what I was told. And I managed to keep out of trouble for the first two years."

"Why did he wait until that night? If he had this plan for you, why then?" My mind is still spinning with the knowledge my police officer stepdad is dirty, and he threatened not just his own son, but both my mom and I.

"I think I know." Mom sighs. "When I overheard that conversation, I found someone I could trust and I can't tell you all the details, but Brian made a mistake that night. He was supposed to be on patrol and watching out for one of the drug runners. But he was distracted. The guy was caught and arrested and the supplier came after Brian because he had broken their deal. A lot of money was lost. Not to mention there was the risk the man arrested would give up names to the police."

"That's why he was home that night early and surprised us, then," I said.

"He had limited time to fix the mistake or his own life would be exposed. That's why he chose that night." Mom clenches her tiny fist and I feel guilty for thinking she was hiding something from me. She's been protecting us both for the past year.

"So what happens now? Dante, you said you'd tell me all this after I had my investor meeting. But now it's out there and I'm still confused why you couldn't have just told me when you came back."

I move quickly over to him and drop to my knees in front of him. That queasy unease is creeping up my spine, like a thousand pinpricks at once. He cradles my face with his hands, the same hands he had to use for his dad's dirty work to protect me. Leaning forward he rests his forehead on mine.

"I was advised to wait until after then, Colbs. I wanted to give up all the names and information I had on my dad that day to make him pay for all of this. Before I could get anything out I was told not to put myself at risk and to be patient."

"But why? What do I have to do with this? I don't understand, D."

My mom clears her throat. "That's why I came without waiting to hear back from you, Colby."

Dante tenses and takes a deep breath.

"That bastard. That fucking bastard!"

The venom dripping from his words does nothing to ease my fears.

"Somebody clue me in, please! What the hell is going on?"

Mom sinks to the floor next to me and takes my hand.

"Colby, your investor meeting...it's with Brian."

"What!? No! That's impossible." I shake my head hard, refusing to hear this, but Mom presses on. "This is why Dante was advised to stay quiet and I just found out a few months ago."

I never wanted to accept help from him when he offered. I went out of my way to do this all by myself. I was so proud of finding my own solution, and now it wasn't even a solution after all.

"Why was Dante told to keep quiet then?"

My mom, bless her for trying to come up with a way to make my simple brain grasp what's going on, but there's no way to soften the words that come out of her mouth.

"Colby, he's been using angel investing loans as a way to launder drug money." She exchanges a glance with Dante. "You're at risk of losing the store."

Letting the words sink in, I scramble up onto Dante's lap and bury my face in his neck.

Chapter 18

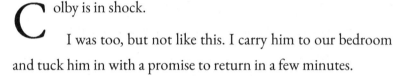

Dante

C olby is in shock.

I was too, but not like this. I carry him to our bedroom and tuck him in with a promise to return in a few minutes.

Hailey still waits in the living room and stands when I enter.

"Is he okay?"

"That's a broad term, but he's in no danger right now. Although I wouldn't be surprised if he gets a migraine tonight. I'll get him to take the good meds before we try to sleep."

"You were always so good to him, thank you."

I shrug, "It's what you do when you love someone, right? Take care of them."

"We'll get through this. Colby will be crushed to lose that store, though. He's worked so hard."

"I'll be there for him. We'll figure it out. He's not going to be charged or anything is he? He didn't know it was dirty money. Will that be held against him?"

If my father somehow got something to stick and he drags Colby down with him, I will hunt him down and hurt him in the worst way I can come up with.

"I've been assured he won't be charged, but all the assets will likely be seized." She sighs. "He'll have to start over."

I study Hailey and the remorse seeps from her. She takes part of the blame for this happening to her son and I don't know how we'll fix this for Colby.

"And what about my father? I don't want details, but you've obviously been working with someone under cover. I didn't spend the last five years of my life on the street and in prison and not learn anything."

She nods with another deep sigh. "I can't risk sharing anything right now, Dante. But it's my hope that he'll be the one behind bars very soon."

"Are you safe? Does he know you're onto him?" I ask softly.

She gathers her things. "I don't think so. But I have... security, so I'm okay."

I open my arms for her and fold her in a hug. I hate that the one person I'm related to by blood is hurting the two people I consider real family so much. Even by doing what I thought was the right thing, it all still happened. It was all for nothing. He made us all suffer anyway.

"He had us all fooled, Dante. Don't blame yourself, okay? I have people on my side and the three of us are going to come through this."

She pulls away and wipes a stray tear away. "Take care of him... son. Don't forget I love you just as much." She reaches up and pats my cheek with her tiny hand. "I thought about you every day you've been gone and I'm so happy you're here."

"Thanks. I'll work towards happy. Right now I'm here and I'm not going anywhere." I walk with her to the door. "Please keep in touch. It's two days until his appointment, are you sure you're okay going back home?"

"I am and I have to. Don't worry about me, okay? You two have enough to take care of."

I make sure she's safely in her car and pulling away before I lock the door and return to the bedroom. Colby lays stiff as a board on the bed staring at the ceiling.

"Colbs, talk to me?" I say gently.

I lay down next to him and grasp his hand. It's softer than mine and I love how his slender fingers fit with my larger rough ones.

"I'm gonna lose my store. All that work for nothing."

My heart breaks at the complete despondence in his voice.

"We don't know that yet. Let's try to stay positive."

He turns his head to me. "You went to prison for nothing. Everything has been for nothing. Because one man happened to charm his way into my mom's life."

I dust the back of my hand down his cheek.

"But it brought me to you. It gave me a woman I love like a mother. It gave me a family and the one person I love above all else." I brush my thumb across his pink lower lip. "We didn't have an easy road to get here, Colby. But we're here. And while the road could've used a warning that the bridge was out, it wasn't for nothing."

His throat bobs with a thick swallow. "I hate that you went through all this for us." His own hand comes up and draws me close for a soft kiss. "And you're right, you're not even close to nothing. You're my everything."

"I'd do it all again for you, you know. There's nothing I won't do for you."

Colby kisses me again and closes his eyes. There's a tiny furrow on his brow as he drops his head to the pillow.

"I'm gonna get you the good meds for tonight, okay? Let's nip this now and try to sleep. It's been a day."

He nods in agreement and before I slip out to get him a glass of water I take a moment to ground myself. So much has changed in the short time I've been out of prison. I never expected all this to happen so fast. Colby I'd hoped would be receptive to have me back, but all this drama with my father I didn't expect.

I shouldn't be surprised he dragged Colby into his money laundering. Why did I even think he'd keep his promise to stay away from him when he was throwing his own son to the wolves without a second thought?

He's underestimated me, though. He won't get to break any of us. Not on my watch.

When I return to the bedroom, Colby is under the covers and sits up to take the pill and water from me before snuggling back down and holding the blanket up in invitation. I strip down to nothing and slide in next to him.

Wrapping him up in my arms and legs, he snuggles against me, every part of him fitting perfectly with me. His breathing evens out, and when I feel the drool on my chest I know he's fast asleep.

I can't join him in the land of dreams, though, and I spend most of the night chasing sleep that never comes.

"Dante! Don't let that fella out!"

I've let my mind wander, and Blaze, one of the ranch hands, snaps me out of my daydream. We're in the north pasture today, earmarking all the spring lambs as well as doing the regular vaccines and check ups on the flock. I manage to pull the gate in time to keep the lamb in while his mom waits anxiously on the other side.

"Sorry," I mumble, but Blaze, I've learned, is not one to let things slide with just an apology. He's going to need an explanation.

He and River, one of the part-time ranch staff, work together quickly to tag the new lamb, give it an injection and record all its info on the iPad in record time. When it's back in the house, the flock data will upload to Dan's cloud and be accessible at any time.

"Break time!" Blaze hollers out, and everyone acknowledges his call, pausing their activity to gather near the shearing shed where we have plenty of coffee and snacks to get through this brutally long day. I used my new phone to text Colby before I left him snoring in bed. He managed to sleep well last night, but I didn't.

"So, Big D, what's on your mind that you can't concentrate and keep a tiny lamb in one place not once, but twice? Were you up late last night gettin' your dick wet or sumthin'?" Blaze says while pulling a cigarette from the pack.

He lights one and inhales deeply. "Fuck, I need to stop smokin', but it's so relaxing. Ever smoke, Big D?"

"A few times. It's not really my thing." I reach for a paper cup near the take out coffee box and fill it. "I prefer caffeine over nicotine, it tastes better."

I muster a smile and he moves in close. Hasn't he heard of the personal space bubble?

"You never answered my question, ya know." His laser blue eyes burn into me and I step back into my own space.

"What question is that?"

"Why are you so distracted? Lady troubles?" As if remembering there's several gay men on the ranch, including his boss, he adds, "Or maybe gentleman troubles, I shouldn't assume."

River snags his own coffee and pipes up. "Gentleman troubles, he and Colby are an item."

Blaze raises an eyebrow. "You up on all the farm gossip are ya, Riv?"

"I'm just saying I know he and Colby are together and maybe that's who he's thinking about. I mean, I can't blame him if he is. Colby's pretty cute. He's got the sun kissed blond hair and those dreamy blue eyes. Looks like he should be on a beach somewhere and not the back of a horse." River drawls out his description of Colby and Blaze's eyes nearly pop out of his head

Blaze removes his hat, scratches his head and reaches for a coffee himself. "You should be a fuckin poet there, Riv. That's some heartfelt shit."

River ducks his head. "Sorry Dante, didn't mean to say all that. I just appreciate a good looking person."

"Uh, no it's fine. You're not wrong. He does look like he should be on a beach some days."

"Did something happen? You look like you didn't sleep well and contrary to what the ever eloquent Blaze says, I don't think it's the kind of tired you get from getting your dick wet."

"My apologies if needed, Big D," Blaze cuts in. "I didn't mean to offend. But what's on your mind? Because I need to know you're not gonna get yourself or anyone else hurt out here by being distracted."

"Remember that time that ewe jumped and you vaccinated me by accident?" River says.

Blaze and River laugh as River rubs at his hand. "Jabbed me right in the meaty part on my thumb! Hurt like a fucker, too. Good news is I didn't need a tetanus shot last year." Blaze frowns as River rubs the spot on his thumb.

"That's the perfect example of why you need to pay attention. So, again, I'm not asking. I'm telling you – spill what's up in your head so we can all stay safe. We may just work together, but we're a team and we help each other. Things can get dicey from time to time on the farm and I need to know you're in the right frame of mind."

As the three of us have been speaking, the rest of the crew arrived for snacks or smoke breaks. Even Alec has returned with Daisy, Dan's border collie who is an amazing herding dog.

"Hey boys." He surveys the three of us close together and the others leaning around. "What's the topic?"

"Dante almost let out two lambs, River thinks Colby is cute, we all need to think and act as a team so we don't get hurt and we still don't know why Big D," he makes air quotes, "is so distracted." A part-timer named Heath provides his summary as he eats a chocolate donut with sprinkles on it. Most of the sprinkles have fallen on his shirt and I wonder if he'll brush them off or eat them later.

Alec pops a piece of gum in his mouth with the same blank expression he always wears.

"Is that true? Are you distracted about something?"

Sighing, I accept this is how it will be today. This ragtag crew of ranch hands won't let us get today's work done until I participate in today's sharing circle. Since I know Alec the best and he's aware of my background, I'm more comfortable to share with this crew. If he's encouraging me, he must trust them.

"Okay, I do have a problem, and it's a big one. I don't know how to fix it and most importantly, if I put this out to you guys it has to remain here."

The group draws closer, nodding they understand. One of them makes a motion to cross his heart, and for a brief moment my throat closes as I survey this motley bunch and realize they truly do want to help me. Not just for work reasons and to be safe, but also because they're kind people. Dan wouldn't hire people who couldn't show compassion for animals and men alike, it's what this whole place is built on. I'm also in no position to be picky for help right now.

The clock is on its final countdown and Colby needs me to come through. So I take a breath and look at Alec. He nods his encouragement and I talk.

And it feels good to do it.

I tell this group of strangers how I went to prison in a misguided attempt to do what's best, how Colby has now been drawn into the whole mess anyway and because his store is linked to a possible money laundering scheme he stands to lose everything. Through it all, they've all listened raptly and drawn closer.

When I finally stop for a breath, Heath speaks up. "To simplify for Dante, if I may, you need a solution to save the store Colby's built up over the last two years and you only have two days before it could potentially go to hell."

How is this guy still eating donuts?

"Um, yes, that's it. No big deal right?" I sigh and sink down on the ground and I'm shocked when Blaze and River do the same. Blaze takes out something that looks like a phone and taps furiously with a stylus. When he notices me watching, he shrugs. "If I don't write it down I'll forget."

"Do you know for sure all his property in the store will be seized?" Alec asks.

"Not yet, no. But from my sources it sounds like a strong possibility. And his emergency fund won't be enough to restart if that's the case. Not to mention the outstanding amount owed, he can't pay that back."

"How much is left, do you know?" Blaze asks.

"I think he said around twenty thousand."

Blaze pecks away again, making notes, and the concentration on his face is intense. He should be a business guy and not some kind of ranch hand. Alec rubs his chin in thought and I feel a small nugget of hope that just maybe, Colby will come out of this only a little bruised and not completely shattered.

"How many doses of vaccine do we have left we need to use today, Blaze?" Alec asks.

"We're on the second bottle so I think twenty?"

Alec booms out the rest of the day's plans. "Fellas, we need to come together to help Colby out of this mess. He'd do it for any one of you and I can't risk having my supplier of surprise bag candy dry up." Light laughter sounds and Alec smiles. "Here's what's going to happen, we need to finish up twenty more vaccines. Secure the area and we'll continue in a few days. Get back to the ranch as soon as possible and come find me. I should be at Dan's."

The guys all get back to their tasks, some going out to round up sheep, others readying the pens and still others start cleaning up all the snacks. Alec clamps a hand on my shoulder.

"Never be afraid to ask this group for help, Dante. I have some ideas I need to talk to Dan about. I'm positive we can work something out for Colby." He mounts his horse and turns back to me. "As soon as Blaze tells you it's okay to come back, take the quad and send your horse back with Heath."

I nod my understanding and return to the group.

"Got yer head in the game now, Big D?" Blaze grins with his teasing, but his eyes are friendly and I relax.

This time when the lamb comes barrelling my way, I catch it easily.

Blaze nods, "It's gonna work out kid, trust me."

Chapter 19

Colby

If I can find a bright side to yesterday's news, it's that I can sleep soundly if I'm wrapped up in Dante. Without him there last night I would've tossed around so much the sheets would be in knots that would make a Boy Scout jealous. Waking up with a clear head after that kind of news is a relief.

Knowing Brian is behind the funding for my store didn't exactly make me warm and fuzzy. Well it did, but that was because I felt like I was going to puke. Once I let reality sink in, I shouldn't have been surprised. Replaying the last few years of my life, since Dante disappeared, I ignored Brian more than usual. It was easy because I was away at college for most of it.

While I was upset I had to rush home and find a home for my horse when Brian decided to move for a promotion and had mom sell the house, I didn't overthink why. I was focused on finding a safe place for Babe and getting back to school. But if I want to be truthful to myself, I suspected something that first Christmas when I came home. It was to their new home two hours away and I was upset I couldn't see Babe without a special trip, but I was also still mourning Dante. I even told my mom it wasn't as fun without him at college and I missed him.

Brian made an offhand remark that night, which I chose to ignore for the sake of my mother. We were watching Christmas movies and I was sitting off on my own while Mom and Brian snuggled. My heart ached for Dante so much that Christmas. Mom was happy I was home and Brian casually mentioned how he makes so much more money in the new position that I should smile more since he made her life better. Mom said she only needed her boys to be happy, money wasn't everything. She didn't notice the shift, but I did. His cold black eyes, nothing at all like Dante's, met mine and I felt like I was in his crosshairs. I had no idea why, though.

The store's rock riff plays and I look up from the papers on my counter. It's a courier with an envelope.

"Are you Colby Calhoun?"

"I am."

He presents the machine for me to sign for it electronically and hands me a legal sized envelope.

There's no return address on it, which is highly unusual. I open it anyway and inside there's a single typed note.

Please bring a certified bank draft for the balance owing to tomorrow's meeting. The loan is being called.

This is the part where I should have a melt down. I should be angry and calling Dante or even Mom, maybe crawling under the blankets too, and hoping it goes away. But you know what?

Fuck. That.

I'd rather lose everything and start over, than be in that bastard's debt.

I had a partial scholarship and money from my dad's life insurance that paid for college. Mom sent me money for spending and to offset my living expenses, but I'm confident it came from her and not him. My car was a student leasing program that Mom co-signed for and I make payments on. Babe has care due to the kindness of Dan and The Broken Horn Ranch that I pay back by volunteering as much as possible and paying for feed as I can.

There's only one reason Brian is the one behind my loan. He wants me to suffer like Dante did. I don't know why, but after I did everything else on my own, he's choosing to pull the rug out from under me when he knows I can't afford it. I'm preparing to expand. I have cost estimates and I even have approval to subsidize wages for a summer student to help run the ice cream expansion. This whole business has been scaling up faster than I ever imagined, and I built it by myself.

He can't take that away from me.

"Shelby, I have to step out for a bit. Will you be okay for an hour or two by yourself?"

Not that I've been doing much but organizing the reports I avoided yesterday. It's nice to ask your employees and not just disappear.

"I should be fine, Colby. Take the time you need."

"Thanks, love. I owe you one."

She laughs and waves her hand for me to leave.

"Nah, but a gal would appreciate a mochaccino should her boss be in the area of The Screaming Bean on his way back."

I laugh, stuffing all my reports in my folder and messenger bag.

"Deal. See you soon."

I'm oddly serene for someone who has less than twenty-four hours to come up with twenty-two thousand dollars somehow. The sun shining on my face, the scent of the lilacs from the trees next to the library and the vision of my future with Dante are a balm to my usually troubled mind. I don't even know if the bank can help me, but I'm sure as hell going to give them a try. The worst they can do is say no, and I can say I tried.

"Hey! Colby!"

My name carries in a voice that sounds vaguely familiar in the spring air.

"Colby! Wait!"

I stand in place as a man in a form fitting navy suit crosses the road towards me. As he draws closer, I gasp when I recognize him.

"Blaze? What are you doing in a suit? I didn't even recognize you."

His smile falls a little when he stops in front of me. "That's the point I suppose. I stopped by the store, but your employee said you left. I took a guess you might be heading this way."

"Yeah, I need to see if anyone will see me on short notice at the bank and I —"

"Can I talk to you before you go in?"

Pausing, I notice now that Blaze is right smack in front of me, he's not wearing an off the rack suit. It's perfectly tailored to him and his shoes are no Walmart specials. Those are brand name dress shoes that probably cost the same as my car payment if not more. Even the watch that glitters on his wrist screams money.

"How did you know I'd be coming this way?"

He hesitates, but only briefly, and I'm mesmerized with this new version of Blaze. He's all confident business man and zero snarky ranch hand. Even his language is businesslike and lacks the laid back drawl I'm used to hearing. There's no jokes or profanity. It's like city Blaze took over country Blaze.

"Dante shared with us the store issue. Please don't be angry about it. I forced him to tell us, okay? I'm in a unique situation to help you and I assumed you might need some assistance with a loan?"

"Ah, okay. Yes, I do and that's why I'm coming to the bank. I'm hoping they can —"

Blaze's strong voice cuts me off and I find myself once again caught up with how different he looks and sounds.

"Colby, I know how banks work. You need me there. And I know you're wondering why I'm standing in front of you in a suit that could pay your rent for a month instead of my jeans, boots and cowboy hat. I can tell you all about me later, but what you need to know right now is that I'm a powerful man with lots of money and I like you. Will you let me help you in there?"

People brush by us on the street and some do a double take at the imposing scene of Blaze in a suit. He's definitely something to be appreciated and I wonder if Dan is aware of his double life. Blaze has been a nice guy to me since we met and I have no reason to not trust him. I probably do need him, but I wanted to do this on my own.

"I know what you're thinking and I promise it will be on your terms, Colby. You can trust me about that."

Puffing out a breath, I know I can't say no to him. "I really wanted to try to find a solution on my own."

Blaze squeezes my shoulder, "It'll be your own solution, you'll just have support to get there. So can I come with you?"

As proud as I am, I'd be a fool to turn him down. If there's any way he can help make this all go down better, I'll take it.

"Please. I'll take the help and I trust you."

With his giant hand on the small of my back he steers me towards the bank. "Let's do this."

The air conditioned quiet of the bank hits us immediately and we approach the smiling woman at the reception desk.

"Hi, my name is Colby Calhoun and I really need to speak to Lewis today."

She smiles her polite customer service smile and my shoulders sag.

"I'm afraid Lewis is unavailable today. I can get you in with him next week at the earliest if you'd like?"

"Excuse me," Blaze makes a show of reading her name tag, "Sharon, Colby has a time sensitive business issue and I'm sure if you checked with Lewis and let him know he's here with his friend Blaze Porter, he'd probably fit us in." He smiles again at her and even I'm caught up in the Hollywood shine of it. "We'll wait if you want to speak to him."

Sharon excuses herself with a smile that's a little warmer and I turn to Blaze. "You've done this before."

"Drop my name when needed? Yes, I have. I don't like to, but sometimes it's needed. I know how the banks work, Colby. Any financial institution for that matter. When you have money, everyone wants to keep it for you. They're looking me up right now and once they figure out who I am, I guarantee Lewis will be seeing us very quickly."

He places one hand in his pocket while he leans his hip against the desk. A perfect GQ pose.

"Um, okay so... who are you really? I know you as the fun and mouthy ranch hand I sometimes bump into when I go riding. You know your way around animals and you tend to work with River a lot." I tilt my head and make a show of looking at him in his suit. "This Blaze?" I wave my hand up and down his body, "I don't know him," I say with a laugh.

He ducks his head. "I don't like many people knowing about this Blaze and I'll tell you more about it later. But... have you heard of BP Technology? PayEx maybe?"

"Oh! PayEx! Yes, that's the company who processes my online order payments for me. It was cheaper than going through my store's point of sale system."

Blaze smiles at me with a raised eyebrow and I get it.

"Holy shit, that's you?"

He fans his hand down his body with a chuckle. "In the flesh." He stands up straight. "Oh, here comes Sharon."

"Sorry to keep you waiting, gentlemen. If you'd like to follow me, Lewis can see you now."

We trail along behind her and I look over at Blaze. *Told ya*, he mouths and I shake my head with a smile. Just when you think you know someone they turn out to be a secret billionaire.

Sharon shows us into an office and Lewis completely ignores me, heading straight to Blaze with his hand extended.

"Mr. Porter, it's a pleasure to meet you. What can I help you with today?"

Blaze ignores Lewis's outstretched hand and presents me instead. "I'm here with Mr. Calhoun. He can let you know what he needs."

I have to give Lewis a little credit for not faltering with his dismissal from Blaze. "Certainly, Mr. Calhoun. What can I do?"

Accepting his limp handshake, I wonder briefly why people pander to the rich. Why can't they just be nice to everyone? I'm Lewis's client, after all.

"I need a business loan for twenty-two thousand dollars and I need it as fast as possible."

"Okay, let's get your information and I'll see what I can do."

Lewis clicks away on his laptop and I fumble with the folder in my bag with all my financials that he may or may not ask for. Blaze is the picture of cool comfort, one ankle resting on his knee as he scans the walls of Lewis's office. His dark scruff is trimmed close today and it's odd to see him without a cowboy hat on. His hair is styled, but if you look close enough you can see the permanent hat head line.

"It looks like you've had your accounts with us for a few years now and your small business Visa is in good standing. What do you need the loan for?"

My mouth goes dry. "I need to pay out a third party lender as soon as possible."

"Oh, so it's an existing debt. Do you have details on interest and payment amounts with you?"

I hand him the sheet of paper I knew he'd need and the only sound in the office is the keys clicking on his laptop. I think I've stopped breathing.

"Do you have any other assets you can offer as collateral? A vehicle or personal savings?"

"My car is leased and everything I own goes back to the store."

Lewis asks me more questions and with each one my heart sinks a little further. He's really not trying to make me feel good about the situation and the constant quiet is telling. I glance at Blaze, but he's still just as uninterested as he was when we first got here.

"I'm afraid with your assets and existing payments, Mr. Calhoun, I can't get the loan approved for you. Your debt service would be too much and the risk is too high."

"But it's replacing a loan payment I already have. I get by okay now."

I twist my bag in my hands.

"I'm happy to hear that, but we just won't take on outside debt like this."

"Excuse me," Blaze interrupts, "What if someone co-signed for him?"

Lewis blinks and stammers his reply. "As long as the co-signer could cover the loan if Mr.Calhoun were to default and their own finances are in good standing, we could re-run the application."

"Can I be a co-signer for you?" Blaze asks.

I wanted it to move fast but now that it is, I feel like I'm lost. "What does it mean for you? Like, do you get statements and know my business and stuff?"

"It means what Lewis just said. If you can't make the payments then it's my debt to take care of. Do you plan on defaulting on the loan, Colby?"

"No," I whisper.

"Good. Lewis, redo it with me as a co-signer please."

Lewis clicks away and I stare at Blaze. He winks and I turn back to see Lewis with a happy smile.

"With Mr. Porter as your co-signer the loan was approved. We can sign everything now and send it for funding, but I don't know if I can get a draft for you by tomorrow. Even with a rush it usually takes three business days."

Blaze waves a hand when he notices my shoulders sag even further. "That's not an issue. As you can see I have the funds in my account. If you can deposit the loan to me when it clears, I can get Colby the draft on our way out. You can do that, right?"

"Yes, absolutely Mr. Porter."

Lewis would most likely do whatever Blaze were to ask at this point. Perhaps even kiss an ass if it were presented.

We sign the loan papers and Blaze ensures I understand the interest and payments and that I'm still paying it back to the bank as I wanted. It's still on my terms and I'm extremely grateful for his help.

We stop at the teller on the way out for a bank draft and he hands it to me.

"Now you're all set for tomorrow."

"Blaze... I don't know how to thank you. Really. I know I'm paying it back, but this is truly incredible."

"Seeing the store remain open is what I want as a thank you. That and a promise for you to carry Tiger Tail ice cream all the time so I'm never disappointed when I drop in."

I manage to return his smile. "I hope it can stay open. They'll likely seize my fixtures and inventory, by what I've read. This loan just makes sure I'm not owing any illegally obtained money, but my stuff was purchased with some of it." Looking skyward, I sigh. "I just have to see how it works out now."

Blaze's lips twitch. "Can I tell you a secret? It's gonna work out, Colby. Never underestimate the good in people and how far your kindness stretches to others."

Blaze extends a hand for me to shake, but I throw my arms around him instead and hug with everything I have. He returns it with just as much force and I have to let go before he cracks a rib.

"You won't regret this, Blaze. I promise."

"I've never made a bad business decision. And I can get Tiger Tail anytime I want. It's win-win."

He apologizes for having to run to another meeting and I remember to swing by the coffee shop for the mochaccino for Shelby.

Here's hoping he's right and it all works out.

Chapter 20

Dante

After the long day and night on the ranch, when I got home Colby was in bed. He'd fallen asleep with a book on his chest and the lamp on. It's the cutest thing I've ever seen. Our last text message was at 10 P.M., so I'm positive he was trying to wait up for me.

The bedroom door's click is like a gunshot in the quiet of the room and I grimace as Colby flutters his eyes open.

"Hey, you."

His sweet, sleepy smile makes my heart flutter.

"Sorry," I whisper. "I didn't mean to wake you."

"S'okay."

He closes his book, placing it on the nightstand, and leans back on his pillows to watch me undress. His gaze roams over every inch of me like a lover's caress, I feel it all the way to my soul.

"I'm gonna have a quick shower." I place a kiss on his forehead. "I'll just be a few, fall asleep again if you have to."

"M'kay. I'll be here."

Chuckling at his persistence to stay awake I rush over to the shower for my nightly routine. The warm water is a godsend on my aching muscles. All the soreness is worth the extra long day, though. Long days and body aches will be the norm until this whole shit storm named Brian passes.

Too many times I wonder if it would have been better if I just said no that night. Maybe things might have been different, or maybe they might have been worse. But I torture myself with it daily. I was supposed to be helping Colby and Hailey when I left. Instead I made it worse. We've all suffered through five years for nothing.

Huffing out a sigh, I shake off the guilt and step out of the shower. The only place I want to be right now is in bed with Colby.

I quickly towel off and open the door to find Landon waiting in the hall. He presses a finger to lips and motions for me to follow him to the living room.

"Hey, Landon. Is everything okay?" I clutch the towel around my waist as Landon seats himself on the sofa. He's completely dressed in his work uniform from the gym still.

"I think so... "

His tone leads me to think it's not. "What happened?"

He scrubs his hands over his face and every minute of sleep he's been missing shows. The circles under his eyes are starting to run circles around themselves. I know we've been caught up in my drama, but what is Landon doing that he looks so damn exhausted?

"I'm almost positive I saw Colby's mom last night." He leans forward, resting his forearms on his knees. "Was she in town?"

"She was here," I confirm. "She showed up unannounced. It threw both of us and her timing was shit." I manage a smile, remembering my mortification at being caught by his mom while we were making out.

Landon smirks. "Sorry about your luck. But was she... alone?"

"She didn't come with my douchebag of a father. Why do you ask?"

Landon chews his lip. The line on his brow deepens and I sit next to him. "Did you see something? Should you tell Colby?"

He shakes his head. "I didn't want to say anything to him just in case I was wrong. But I'm positive I saw her in a car with another man when I went to the diner tonight. I parked at the back since there were no spaces out front and there was another car back there. Do you know the back parking lot of the diner at all?"

I shake my head no. It's been a long time since I've even been to a restaurant let alone the parking lot of one.

"Well, in the back there's only one light fixture and it's near the building since that's where most people park. At the back of the lot it gets dark. I've told them they should install more lights for safety but that's never happened. Anyway, the guy opened the door and when the interior lighting came on I saw her."

"She was with someone who wasn't my dad?"

He nods. "Yeah, but I didn't recognize the guy at all."

"Do you want me to tell Colby?"

"I don't know. I was going to call him today but something told me I shouldn't." He runs his hands through his hair. "But I don't like keeping things from him, either."

I lean back and think of what Hailey told me before she left. She said she had security and was safe. Maybe it was a bodyguard?

But she also said she was going back home and didn't. What is she leaving out?

"Keep it quiet until tomorrow. Things are about to get messy, I think."

Landon sits up with a start. "Do I need to do anything? Is he okay?"

I allow myself to smile. "I think he's going to come out okay." I stand up, adjusting my towel again. "Will you be okay?"

"Me? I'm fine. Just a long day and this was really bothering me. It's not like Hailey to be meeting strange men in a dark parking lot."

"I'll let you know if I hear anything. Thanks for telling me."

I leave Landon, finally, and get back to where I really want to be. When I open the door this time, Colby has the lamp off and his book on the table, but he's still awake.

"Was Landon going all big brother on you? I heard voices." His sleep thick voice greets me and I'm happy he's still awake. Even if it's just to share a few quiet moments together.

He slides over to give me room and I wrap myself around him. There's no better feeling than having Colby next to me. Okay, having him in me would be a great feeling too, but nothing feels better than this. He still smells like strawberry mint shampoo and his soft skin is like smooth butter against my own rough exterior.

"He just wanted to make sure you were okay and I was treating you well." I skim my nose softly against his. "I told him I treat you like a prince and he was good with it." Laughing softly I feather a kiss on his lips.

"I don't need a royal treatment, you know. I just need you." He rests his head on my chest and I let my fingertips skim up and down his spine. He may not want any royal treatment, but I'll make sure he gets the best of everything. "Speaking of royals, did you know Blaze is a rich dude?"

My body shakes with a laugh. "I didn't until this afternoon when he pulled me aside and told me his plan. I guess he found you and it worked out?"

He kisses my chest again and I savour this simple moment. I could have this and nothing else every day and be happy. "He did, and I have the bank draft for tomorrow. Blaze is a force in a suit though. Wow."

"Do I have competition?" I tease.

"Nah. The only suit I like you in is your birthday suit."

Colby snort laughs and I join him.

"God, you're cheesy."

My eyelids are heavy. As they should be after today, and tomorrow is gearing up to be just as long. Colby will need me, I'm sure of it.

"D?"

"Yeah?"

"I'm really nervous about tomorrow." His finger tip traces an invisible pattern on my chest.

"I know you are. Do you need me to go with you?"

His hair tickles my chest as he shakes his head. "No. I have to do this myself, I'm just scared of what's going to happen to my store."

"It's going to work out, Colbs. I spent the last five years holding on to hope I'd get back to you. I'm not about to lose hope for your store. We'll make it work." Kissing his head I squeeze him tighter to me. "Get some sleep, k?"

With a kiss to my chest, he squeezes me back and somehow we both manage to sleep.

Mittens and I are in a deadlock.

She refuses to eat and I refuse to give up.

But too many days have passed and if she won't take food today, we'll need to call the vet to intervene. She moved from her corner at some point since I had to clean her pen. I'm certain she took some hay from the trough, but not much. I'd like to turn her into the pasture and see if that's the issue but I can't keep as close an eye on her if I do that.

Fuck, I know nothing about llamas. All I've done is google a million different llama sites and panic because she's not eating enough. This damn animal shouldn't cause me so much stress.

"Mittens, I'm about ready to break over here. You gotta give me something, girl."

I'm shocked to hear a break in my voice, and maybe Mittens is too. She twitches her ears and turns her head, her giant brown eyes and extra long eyelashes blink at me. I don't know if she's finally given up being stubborn or maybe she feels my genuine concern for her well being. Whatever it is, it's working because she turns her whole body to face me and takes a step in my direction. I'm leaning against the side of the pen with my head in my hands after yet another snub at eating the special llama grain I picked up. She eyes the cat dish full of feed and takes a bite.

I don't even want to breathe in case something changes. She eats the little dish of food and stands there chewing while watching me. She takes a few more steps and now stands in front of me, close enough to touch. Slowly I extend my hand out, palm flat and she dips her nose to sniff it. Her nose is soft and it tickles my palm. She seems insulted that there's no food there.

"Do you like carrots?"

I found the stash of carrots in the horse barn and have one in my pocket as a last resort today. I snap off a piece and she leans her head over now, trying to get a glimpse of what I'm doing.

"Just a small piece for now, girl. I'm not sure how much you should have."

She takes the carrot piece gently and crunches it down. While she eats I pet her neck and reach up to scratch her ears. She pauses her chewing and hums.

"Do you like your ears scratched?" I reach up to do it again and she pushes her head into my hand.

My smile feels like it might break my face in two. I wonder if Mittens knows how much I needed this to happen today? I keep feeding her the carrot and when she's done, she waltzes over to the trough and eats more of the hay I've left for her. My relief to see her eat is so great I could cry.

Footsteps sound in the barn and Blaze appears, leaning on the rail with me.

"I didn't want to interrupt the moment. How are you feeling?"

"About Mittens? So fucking relieved. Dan had faith I'd get her to come around, but I was doubting if she would." I wipe at my wet eyes. "I'm tearing up over a llama eating. Stupid animal."

Blaze nods and turns away while I get myself under control. Not that I'm ashamed to show emotion, I'm just... overwhelmed.

"I think she knew I really needed her to come through, you know?"

Blaze nods. "I think animals can know those things. It's what I love about rescue animals and when you make that breakthrough. It's like they see you for the nice human you are and they know you can help them. You're not like the other people they've met. It's scary and satisfying all at once. That trust they have in you and you hope you never let them down."

Something tells me Blaze is talking about a lot more than animals. But it definitely fits what's going on in my life on all accounts.

"Colby told me you were able to catch him yesterday. He said you fill out a suit well." I laugh, surprised to see Blaze blush.

"I know it's a shock to see me in anything other than jeans and t-shirts, but I wouldn't get the same respect in a place of finance if I walked in like this." He tugs at his stained t-shirt with a smile. "I hate making those kinds of appearances, but sometimes you just need to if you want things to happen your way."

I know too well what he means.

"Colby's meeting with his stepdad, my father, scum of the land, in a few hours." I swallow hard. The anxiety of this meeting has been gnawing away at me and I want desperately to waltz in there and rip my father's balls out through his throat for doing this, not just to me, but to Colby and Hailey too.

Blaze nods in understanding. "I came to let you know if you want to do something else to get your mind off it, River has some of the younger lads in the shop helping him build shelving. You can still feel like you're helping that way instead of stewing over it. Or you can stay and talk to the llama. Dan has no other chores for you today, he got others to cover it."

"I could've done my work today, I'm not sick."

He lays his hand on my arm and I'm forced to look into his face. "Dante, this isn't just a place to come and work to get paid. Dan and I go way back and one thing we always agreed on is you look after the people who work for you. You're not just a ranch hand. You're part of this motley bunch we call family." He squeezes my arm before releasing me. "We don't know how it feels to go through what you and Colby are, but we do know how it feels when we have no one to turn to. We don't like that feeling, so please let us help."

I turn my attention to Mittens, wondering if she's okay and if I should stay to comfort her more or if I should join them in the workshop. Blaze's footsteps echo out of the barn and once I know he's gone I fold my arms and rest my head on them. The stew of all the different emotions raging right now is hard to contain and I don't know what I should do.

A small nudge to my head has me lift my head and Mittens stands there, still chewing.

"You think I should go up there? Will you be okay and keep eating?"

Mittens rips a giant mouthful out of the trough with a look. *I'm eating just fine, go!*

With a laugh, I promise to return later and I walk up to the workshop, desperate to stop worrying about Colby.

Chapter 21

Colby

Once Shelby arrived for her shift I retreated to my back room to get my thoughts together.

What the hell was I going to do or say to Brian? Throw the bank draft at him and tell him to fuck off? Beg him to not hurt my mother? Punch him for hurting us all anyway, especially for what he did to his own son?

All the documents I prepared for this meeting lay on the loveseat. When I thought I was meeting someone who was stepping up to mentor me, perhaps help me with my expansion even, I was excited to look at a spreadsheet. Let it be known, I loathe spreadsheets, so this was a big deal. Now they're a reminder that everything I've worked for is about to be crushed into a thousand tiny pieces.

My guts churn thinking about what happens next. I know I can get my old part time job back if needed. I called the brewery and spoke to the owner, Dylan, today. Knowing I'll be able to pay my half of the rent takes a load off my mind. Dante works and I know he'll contribute until I can figure out how to start up the store again if the worst should happen.

I'm trying to remain positive that paying off Brian will be the end of it, but I don't see how I won't lose everything in this building since it's tied to a dirty money scheme. Ignorance about where the money came from is no excuse.

Cracking a ginger ale from my mini fridge, I gulp it down and hope it settles my stomach. Although at this point I don't think I'll be leaving the nauseous feeling behind until I actually throw up. Tucking the bank draft into my wallet, I take a final scan of my little back room of comfort and wonder how much longer it will be mine.

"I have my financial meeting and I don't think I'll be back after. Can you lock up tonight?" I ask Shelby before I leave.

Shelby smiles and nods yes, and the knot in my stomach grows. It's not just me losing out, she's losing employment too. The fact she's blissfully unaware of that does nothing to help me feel better about it and I quickly slip out before I say something I can't explain.

I'm not meeting Brian in a bank. Why would I? Now that I know he's been laundering money for years he wouldn't want this kind of business occurring in a bank. Instead I'm meeting him in a shared office work space downtown in Bloomburg. It's a space many people who work at home visit to network in and to feel like they're part of a larger environment. There's open office areas, boardrooms and even a kitchen area with refreshments.

As my feet carry me closer to the building I duck into a small alley to take a breath and text Dante.

Colbs: The meeting is in the shared office space building downtown in fifteen minutes. If I don't call you in an hour, please call me instead.

Colbs: I didn't get to tell you I loved you this morning either, so I guess I am now.

Colbs: *heart emoji*

I know Dante sometimes works where there's no cell service on the ranch or he doesn't have the phone set to buzz, so I'm not worried that he doesn't answer me and I stuff the phone back in my pocket. What worries me is the lack of activity in the usually busy building. There's always a few people working on laptops in the open meeting area, but right now there's not a soul to be found.

Stepping into the usually bustling place, the quiet is impossibly loud, and goosebumps run up my arms. A rattle comes from the utility room and a maintenance man exits with tools and a mop bucket.

He nods a hello and tilts his head. "Did you not know the power will be out here in about an hour? We have to do some work on the electrical panel."

That explains the lack of people then.

"Oh, no, I didn't. But I won't be long. I'm meeting someone in room C then I'll be out of your way."

My footsteps echo in the empty building and with each squeak of my shoe that brings me closer to room C, my stomach is more insistent that it needs to evacuate the contents. I know Brian, well I thought I did. We've shared a roof, we've eaten dinner together and he married my mother. While he was never the warm father figure I hoped he would be, I never felt the same threat from him like Dante did.

Until now.

Now it feels like I'm about to walk into a pit of rattlesnakes.

Filling my lungs with a fresh gulp of air, my sweaty palm turns the knob on the door. At first I only see an empty desk, but the rustling of fabric draws my gaze to the right and my stomach tightens.

"Colby, on time as always."

He buttons his blazer in the front and flashes his too white smile. He should offer sunglasses to people, it's so blindingly white. Why is he wearing a blazer in June?

"What are you doing here?" I finally manage to ask, but he tilts his head in that condescending way I instantly hate.

"Colby," he chides, and I clamp my teeth down so hard he probably heard them click together. "Don't play dumb. You knew I'd be here." He pulls out the chair from the desk and motions for me to sit in one of the chairs in front of it. I gingerly sit as indicated and make sure I'm a safe distance away from him.

"Why do you say that?"

"Did you honestly think your business plan would attract a legitimate investor?" He smirks, and I know he's trying to push my buttons.

"It's a solid plan and you've been seeing the numbers for several years. It's a profitable business."

He smirks again. "Hmm, indeed it has been. I was almost impressed by it. But I need to take the cash and invest in something that will turn the funds over faster. When you start to grow a business as big as I do, the money needs cleaning a lot faster. If you know what I mean."

He flashes his over bleached smile again and I want to punch him in the throat.

"Why did you call the loan if you could see the business is doing so well? If your so-called business is growing so fast my measly twenty-two thousand isn't enough for you to worry about. You probably have bigger clients than me."

He peers at me, his nose scrunched like he just had a whiff of something rotten.

"Ah, yes, well that's easy. Because I'm a bit of a bastard and I can. No other reason." He laughs like he told the world's best joke and I wonder what my mom ever saw in this man. "Well, and someone else might benefit from it now, so I like to spread it around."

I want to punch him in the face, no, I want to kick him in the face and watch all his too white teeth fall to the floor in a rain of tiny Chicklets. Then I want to do it again for what he did to Dante.

"What if I can't pay you?"

His dark laugh sends chills racing down my spine. I wonder if that's the same laugh Mom heard?

"It's not an option. You pay it or I make you pay. And you don't want me to make you pay." He leans back and the chair squeaks in protest.

"You already made me pay." I whisper, and immediately wince at how weak and helpless I sound. He pounces on it.

"Are you whining about Dante leaving you high and dry? Please, get over it. He did what he had to, to save himself. It wasn't about you, you know. You always were so fucking sensitive. Dante didn't need you in his life. He had the chance to make a lot of money in that little drug ring and he took it." His lip curls as he glares at me.

I swallow back the bile. He's a liar and he knows it.

"It's not sensitive, asshole. It's called being human and caring about people. Something you have no capacity to do," I spit back.

"Watch your mouth, boy." He sneers. "You have no idea what I've had to deal with. Caring is a waste of effort and it's for the weak. The only person you should look out for is yourself. The sooner you learn that, the smoother your life will be."

"Do you speak to my mother like that?"

His smirk returns when he notices my clenched fists.

"You mean she hasn't told you how I talk to her?"

My heart races. "What do you mean?"

"Colby, stop with the games. Your mom obviously came to see you recently. Did she not share our arrangement with you?"

I continue to stare at him with his smug smirk and I see no obvious sign he's lying to me. But I know my mom would never, ever put him over me.

"Ah, so she didn't tell you. Interesting." He folds his hands over his chest. "So where's the money, Colby? Are you paying me today or are you going to make it difficult?"

"If I pay you today, you'll leave me alone? And Dante?"

He scoffs. "I couldn't give a rat's ass about Dante. Kid couldn't even make a drug drop without getting caught. The only thing that got him back to you was not telling the lawyers who sent him on that run. If he would've been smart and made that delivery he would've been set for life." He stares off into the distance and I wonder if he's thinking about what could have been for him or for Dante. Something tells me Brian was hoping to use Dante as his own personal springboard to some other kind of dealing and it makes my skin crawl.

Reaching into my pocket, I pull out my wallet and unfold the bank draft. I will my fingers to stop shaking and by some miracle they do as I toss the paper on the desk, not wanting to get close enough for a hand off.

Brian picks it up and scans it before tucking it into the pocket on his blazer. When he does I glimpse a gun in a holster at his side. I don't know anything about guns, but it doesn't make sense for him to wear a gun on a day he's not at work. I don't want to stick around any longer to find out what he's up to, either.

"If that's all, then I'd like to get going."

His cold stare stays on me and this time the bile actually does rise in my throat.

"When you see Dante tell him good old Dad said hello, will you?"

"I'm not delivering any message from you," I spit. No way in hell would I do any request from this man, no matter how simple. "And he wouldn't want it anyway."

He rises from the chair, a sly smile sliding onto his face.

"You could always come work for me instead, you know. Leave Dante hanging so he knows how it feels to be left for money."

"Go fuck yourself."

I hurry to the door, desperate to no longer share the air with him. Flinging the door open too hard, it bounces off the wall and his amused laughter rings out. All I want to do is put distance between me and this puke ball. I need to hug Dante and Babe and just get somewhere to process it all.

And I should probably call my mom to tell her it's done. As I pull out my phone to look at the screen, I crash into a strong, broad chest.

"Oh I'm so sorry. I wasn't paying attention," I mutter and try to step around, but firm hands on my arms don't let me go. It's the maintenance man from earlier.

"No problem. I was coming to tell you your car needs to move. It's blocking the lane."

My brow furrows. "I didn't drive –"

"Your car, the red one, it's blocking the lane."

Nothing about this whole exchange is normal. The man's eyes plead with me to go to my car that I didn't bring and for some reason, I listen and do as he says.

"Oh, I'm so sorry. I'll move it right now."

Rounding the corner to the lane, there's no red car but there's a van with an electrical company's name on the side and while it should be giving me stranger danger vibes, it doesn't. I walk up to it and the side door slides open by someone I never expected to see here.

"Mom!? What's going on?"

I feel like I just walked into another dimension. It's not an electrician's van, it's an observation van and there's two guys watching close circuit cameras of the room I was just in with Brian. With their head phones I'm assuming they heard everything too.

"Colby, this is attorney Sheldon Scott. He's been... helping me. Helping us."

A middle aged man with very kind eyes extends his hand.

"Hi Colby, I've heard a lot about you from your mom. She's been a great help to our investigation."

Seriously, this is the twilight zone.

"Mom?"

There's a commotion on the screen and one of the men with headphones rips them off with a curse. "I'm going in for backup. Call the cars."

Mom tugs me out of the way as Mr. Scott pulls out a cell phone and the other man calls for assistance at our location. Almost immediately I hear sirens.

"What the fuck is going on, Mom?" My voice wavers and I just want to get out of here.

Adding to the chaos, my phone goes off and my hands fumble to accept the call from Dante.

"Colbs? It's been an hour and I was worried when I hadn't heard from you."

"I'm okay. I'm ah... in a van with Mom and Mr. Scott and I think they're arresting Brian."

A garbled sound comes across the line and I know Dante is struggling to keep it together.

"D, everyone is okay. I want to come out there and see you and Babe. Can you get her into the stall for me? No ride, I just need you both."

His voice is thick. "Anything for you, Colbs. Be careful and come as soon as you can."

"I will."

Stuffing the phone into my pocket, I return my attention to my mom and Mr. Scott.

"I know there's a lot of questions to be answered here. But I... I just... I need to be with Dante now. Can I go?"

Mom looks at Mr. Scott and he nods. "Nothing we need is pressing. Your mom and I will call you tonight and go over everything."

I nod and stumble out of the van. There's three police cruisers in front of the building and Brian is being forced into the back of one. While it's a gratifying image, I need to get to Dante.

With the thought of him in my head, I jog as fast as I can back to my car at the store.

Chapter 22

Dante

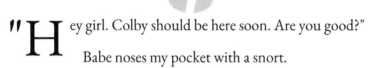

"Hey girl. Colby should be here soon. Are you good?"

Babe noses my pocket with a snort.

"No more treats until Colbs is here, okay?"

She puffs her warm breath along my neck and swishes her tail impatiently, but she knows. Like any animal who is loved, she's aware her people are stressed and she doesn't press her luck by using her size to muscle more carrots out of me.

I could always count on finding Colby with his horse if he had a bad day. Or if I couldn't find him, I knew he'd be with her. I'm not afraid to admit I was jealous of a horse. Funny thing is, this horse is what brought us together. She gave me the courage to tell Colby how I felt about him, and since that day of whispered confessions and tentative kisses, Babe has been in my mind almost as much as Colby.

Leaning into her, I press my head against her strong neck and breathe.

It's all going to be okay.

A shadow falls at the doorway and I turn from the stall to find Colby. He's a gorgeous mess with his blond hair in disarray and trying so hard to keep his emotions in check. His blue eyes seek mine and I curse my father for causing pain to this kind and beautiful person. He couldn't just leave it alone and be happy with fucking my life up, he needed to make sure Colby suffered too. His throat bobs and he chews his lower lip as he tries to speak and fails.

"Colbs, c'mere."

He crosses the distance in a few steps and collapses in my arms. Tremors shake his slight frame and I never want to see him this upset again. His fingers flex and claw at the fabric of my shirt as he works his way towards forming words. But there's no rush, we have all the time in the world for him to tell me what happened.

His body finally stops vibrating and he releases his grip on my body, instead taking my hand and drawing me farther into the stall with Babe. Her ears twitch and she softly snickers when Colby wraps his arms around her neck. The soft puffs of her breath make his hair fly up and she rubs her head against his. This is what always made me wish I was a horse when we were teenagers. Specifically this horse. I wanted so badly for him to show me the same affection he did with Babe.

Stepping forward I slide a hand on his back as I run the other one down Babe's. "I love that you have a horse like this to share your bad days with. I wish I was this horse sometimes." I swallow, not knowing if he'll remember that's what I said to him that day or not. But I should know by now, Colby will never disappoint me.

He lifts his head, his blue eyes so sad, but a small smile plays at his lips. "That's funny, because sometimes I wish this horse was you."

"I think you're really cute." My smile grows as we play out this scene from a time so long ago. The night that forever changed my relationship with Colby.

"Really?" He turns away from Babe, placing a hand on my chest. "I think you're hot."

He bites his lip, just like that day and I can't help but stray from the script.

Taking his gorgeous face in my hands I kiss him gently. "I'm going to skip ahead a little and just kiss you. Because I fucking love you and you need to know we're gonna make this work."

Pressing my lips to his he kisses me back with more force than I expected, and when he pulls away, the fire in his eyes makes any more words die on my tongue.

"We'll figure it out. I have you back and I'm never letting you go. Five fucking years, Dante. He stole it from you and he stole it from us." He slides his fingers through my hair. "I won't let him win and I won't let you go. You belong with me. And Babe." His shoulders relax and his kiss is more tender this time before he turns to grab a brush and start grooming Babe. Another habit he has when he needs to calm down or think. I suspect right now it's a little of both so I pick up a brush and work the other side of her.

I don't question him about what happened and enjoy the comforting silence of us doing this task together, just like old times. Babe likes it too.

"He was arrested today when I was leaving. I saw it." Colby's voice is flat. "He was being monitored. My mom was helping the police with an attorney, Sheldon Scott."

I stare at Colby. "He's the crown attorney I went to see. The one who told me to wait and not come to him until after your meeting."

Colby gazes at me over the back of Babe before going back to brushing. "So Mom's been working with him for a while and knew what happened to you. They need to talk to me tonight. I was free to come here but I have to go back and find out what's next."

I remain quiet. With Hailey's parting comments about having protection and her skirting my questions, I knew she was likely working with someone. I didn't expect it would be with Mr. Scott, though. She came through for both of us, it seems.

"When do you need to be back?" I ask.

"I said I'd be home when you were done with work. I want you there with me. It affects you too."

"Say the word and I'll let Dan know. We'll take one car back if that's okay? I don't want you driving like this."

Colby nods and keeps brushing Babe. She's loving the extra grooming, but the furrow in his brow tells me he's still trying to process. Putting my brush in the bin, I come around to Colby and rub my hand up his back. "I'll go find Dan or Alec and let them know. Take your time."

"Thank you," he whispers.

With a kiss to his cheek I leave him with his horse to find one of my bosses. They already know I'll be leaving, but Colby needs time alone.

And I need time to process that my father has been arrested and I might finally be able to start the life I lost five years ago.

Chapter 23

Colby

Sometimes we never know what we're capable of until we're pressed so close to the wall our only choice is to kiss it and accept it for what it is. An obstacle we have to overcome.

Dante drives my car home as I blankly stare out the window. I'm not noticing much outside because my mind is a blender of thoughts and emotions. Any words to describe how I feel keep passing through the sieve. No words want to hang back for the job. Well, there's a few words, but they seem inadequate.

Devastated.

That's the best word I can find to express how I'm feeling. Not just for myself, but for Mom and Dante too. My mom thought she found her next true love with Brian. To hear her speak about Dad, it seemed like love would never be possible again and Mom would be single forever. Not that she minded, but even a ten-year-old boy can sense when their parents are missing something. When she met Brian she had that happy glow back I hadn't seen for a long time. He made her happy and in turn, it made me happy.

He brought a son the same age as me with him and while it took awhile to get to know the son, he became my closest friend and eventually my true love. Because not even five years apart erased him from my heart. One man made three different people incredibly happy until one day, he tore it all down. Devastated was how I felt waking up to learn Dante was gone that day and it's how I feel now, knowing Brian wasn't just a passive participant, but actively working to tear our worlds apart.

I don't know if any of us will ever know why he did it, either. It scares me to know such wicked people exist.

Dante reaches over and his firm hand squeezes my knee. His thumb soothes gentle caresses in the familiar motion of comfort with the message he's here for me. It's only this week I've realized, even when he was gone, he was still here for me. Because I never allowed my heart to let him go. Even when my mind decided it was time to move on, it couldn't.

By keeping him close, my memories got me through stressful times just as much as they kept me up at night missing his gentle touch. Every time I groomed Babe like we did tonight, I replayed that scene when we lived it the first time. It was the purest and sweetest moment of my life, and even though I missed him, I wasn't ready to let him go no matter what my mind wanted to do.

Glancing at his profile, his sharp jaw is set as he drives and I know he's not looking forward to the conversation to come either. None of us are coming out of this unscathed.

But there's another word I've managed to pull from the blender, and it's hope. It's just a tiny pebble, but I'm choosing to focus on that over anything else. Everyone keeps saying it's all going to work out, like the Magic 8 Ball said so and it must be true. Blaze helped already and told me it would work out. Dante seems hopeful it's all going to work, even if he's just as bruised as I am. Even this Mr. Scott guy seems to think it's going to work out, by what he told Dante.

That much positivity has to mean something, right?

My mom's car is parked in front of the house already and Dante takes our spot in the driveway. He kills the engine and turns towards me.

"Are you feeling okay? Is there a headache starting?" He soothes his hand on my thigh and I get lost in those soulful brown eyes.

"No headache." Licking my lips I grasp his hand in mine and squeeze. "Thank you for asking." My voice hitches as he leans across the console to brush a kiss to my temple.

"You never have to thank me for taking care of you."

"I can't stop because it means more than you'll know."

"I do know, Colbs. Because you allowing me to do it means just as much to me. I can't tell you how privileged I feel to be the one taking care of you." He releases a shaky breath and squeezes my thigh harder. "All I ever wanted was to be there for you. It's been a long time."

I sigh a shaky breath. I don't think it's possible for me to love anyone like I do him. "Let's do this, then, and keep taking care of each other."

Dante kisses me softly on the lips and his tender gaze feeds me the courage I need for the conversation ahead. A car door closes and my gaze shifts outside. My mom and Mr. Scott have exited the car and walk towards us. Dante and I meet them on the front porch and it's not until we're inside my mom engulfs me in a fierce hug.

"Colby, I feel terrible having kept all this from you for the last year. But I hope once we explain you'll understand and forgive me."

Hugging her back I whisper, "I don't think there's anything to forgive, Mom. I just want to understand."

She releases her hold and wipes a tear from her cheek. "I'm just happy to have both my boys back."

Dante has already invited Mr. Scott to sit and he takes the recliner. Mom sits on the loveseat next to him and I sit next to Dante on the sofa. Again his hands rests on my thigh and I place my hand over top of his.

Mr. Scott breaks the silence. "I know this didn't play out exactly as we hoped, but in the end it's mostly good."

"Mostly good. Right. I'd like it all from the beginning if we could," I manage to speak, my voice hoarse.

My mom glances at Mr. Scott and he nods. She picks up where she left off the other night.

"I told you I had overheard Brian on the phone when I was here last. It made me second guess everything he'd ever told me about Dante's disappearance." She fidgets with the cuff on her shirt. "I went to the library one night after work and used their computers in case he was on to me and ever searched my computer. The first thing I did was look up missing person cases that were still open."

Dante's hand squeezes mine and mom's gaze drops to our hands. "You want to tell us why you called the police to say you weren't missing?" Her voice is soft, not judging Dante. She knows why, but she's asking for him to tell it his way.

He flexes his fingers in my thigh and I squeeze back.

"After he dropped me off that night, I was making drug deliveries two nights later. On the third night when I met the receiver he, ah, knew that report was out and accused me of putting the operation at risk. My face would be out there and I could be noticed and draw unwanted attention." He swallows hard. "He hit me so hard my eye swelled to the size of a baseball and said I needed to get the report cancelled asap or they'd make Dad pay for his fuck up." He rushes on. "And I really wanted to ignore him so they would make him pay, but that brought it all back too close to you two. So I called the number and spoke to someone and confirmed I was okay. Since I was over eighteen there was no runaway report needed either. It just got closed and filed away so that I wasn't missing."

"And we just assumed it was an open case all those years. I would never have thought to look into that," I whisper.

Dante turns his sad smile to me. "I know, it's not your fault."

Mom tucks her feet under her, hugging a throw pillow to her chest. "When I learned the report had been closed for years I did some investigating. It took me awhile, but I found a court entry with Dante's name versus the crown and no other details. Which backed up the comment Brian made and confirmed he knew Dante was in jail. So I found the name of the attorney on the case and that's where Sheldon comes in." Mom turns to Mr. Scott who she's on a first name basis with and his returning expression to her makes me wonder if Mom found more than an attorney.

"When your mom came to meet with me, the timing couldn't have been better. As you already know, Brian was involved with some shady characters and he's been under our watch for quite some time. But we couldn't catch him doing enough to arrest him and make it stick. He was very careful at keeping himself far enough away from the activity to not get caught. We knew he was working with some drug dealers, smaller ones for kick backs while on duty, but we wanted to connect him to the big guy."

Mom leans forward. "If I knew what he'd done sooner, Dante, I would've looked for you. You didn't deserve this and I'm so sorry."

Dante offers a small smile. "I know and it's okay, Hailey. Nobody knew this about him, not even me, so don't blame yourself."

"But you knew something was off with him, ever since you were a boy. You told me that you never felt he was a good person," I say.

"That's right. But I just thought he maybe never wanted to be a parent, or he just resented having to care for me. I didn't ever expect my father to be a crooked cop and into dealing drugs." He shakes his head. "I could never have imagined this scenario."

Mr. Scott continues. "With the help of your mom, we were able to connect him to the money laundering side of it. He was a police officer making far more than his salary and there was only so much we could do legally to gather evidence. Even we have to follow the law for evidence gathering. He did a fantastic job layering the funds and making them almost impossible to track." His blue eyes set on me. "Until he made a mistake."

"I never went through Brian's things, ever, in our fifteen years of marriage. I trusted him. He loved me and you, Colby. At least he did at one point. I refuse to believe we were all just used by him." Mom's voice hitches and she takes a moment to breathe. "But I went through his office one night when he was at work and found some documents, and... that's when I knew he was just being mean for the sake of it and he wasn't the man I met that night at the wine bar. He wasn't the same man who, when the heel of my shoe broke, carried me to the car instead of letting me walk barefoot on the sidewalk. And he wasn't the same man who went out at 2 A.M. to find more popsicles when you were crying with a fever and strep throat and it was all you could eat." Mom loses the battle as tears flow freely down her cheeks and my heart breaks for her. "That man was gone and I gave the information to Sheldon."

I hand Mom a tissue and lean in to hug her. "Mom," I croak. I hate seeing my mother cry and I hate more that there's nothing I can do about it.

"Your mom found a document for a transaction that connected the dots and gave us enough evidence to pursue Brain for money laundering." I sit back down next to Dante as Mr. Scott continues. "Colby, Brian owns the building you rent. Your rent was going to an account for a numbered company and that account was already flagged by us. When your mom came to me with proof he was also behind your loan, it was enough for us to keep pulling information on other dealings. It's been slow, but we were about to move in to arrest him when Dante paid me a visit. It's why I urged Dante to not step forward with any names, we were going to take him down this way and hope he'll give us what we want."

"You want him to make a deal and give you dealer names? If he bargains, how long could he be in for?" Dante grates, and his squeeze on my hand is impossibly tight.

"We'd still ask for the maximum he could get and it would depend on the judge. We're hoping we can use protective custody within prison as a bargaining chip instead."

The silence hangs heavy and I turn to Mom. "He said something to me today. Didn't your mother tell you how I talk to her? What did he mean?"

She once again checks with Mr. Scott before answering. "About a month ago he hinted he knew I was onto him and I told Sheldon immediately because he threatened me."

I try to express my anger, but she holds up a hand to stop me.

"It was scary, yes, but I wasn't about to let him get to me. And like Dante, he knew my weakness was you. I wasn't letting him manipulate me. I knew he still had to be careful. He did his best to make it difficult for me though. He locked me out of our shared bank account and changed the locks on the house."

"Where have you been staying!? Oh my god Mom, are you safe?"

She smiles and for the first time I see relief and maybe a touch of happiness. "I've been in a safe house with a guard for a while as a precaution, but I can go back to the house now. I'm perfectly fine, Colby. Sheldon insisted I keep a bodyguard around for a bit longer just in case, but I'm okay."

When my anger at the threat to my mom dissipates, I return to what Mr. Scott said about my building. There's too many shocks at once and it's finally dawning on me the severity of all this and the future of Lick It Up.

"He owns my building?" God I feel sick. He took my rent and my loan payment, both sums going back to feed whatever his current illegal activity is. This can't be good. "What happens now?"

Mr. Scott puffs out a sigh and the remorse on his face doesn't give me the warm and fuzzies. "The tenants of the building will be informed and as a business you'll be shut out. I'm sorry."

"Do I get to go in one last time? Is everything going to be taken, too?" My voice cracks and Dante's weight leans into me.

"I can accompany you tonight if you'd like, but... I can't let you take anything. Until the trial is over everything is seized." He sighs again. "I'm really sorry Colby, but I can't do anything more than that."

I can only nod and hang my head, staring at the old throw rug Landon and I bought at a flea market last summer. Life was a lot more simple then.

But now my store, my second home, is lost. It's a part of my heart and a part of me. Every shelf and piece of decor and candy in there brought me life every day. I built it and now it's gone.

"I think I'd like to do that. Can Dante be with me?"

Mr. Scott nods. "Of course. Just tell me when you want to go."

"Now?"

I look at Dante and he nods in agreement as we stand.

Mom stays behind and the three of us load into my car and head to Lick it Up.

One last goodbye to everything I built.

Chapter 24

Dante

Watching Colby move around his store for what was probably the last time is a new kind of heartbreak.

I keep a respectful distance, as does Mr. Scott, as Colby runs his fingers over the displays and smiles sadly at the custom built lollipop stand. It's painted bubblegum pink and it's nothing more than an oversized piece of dowel with holes drilled for the sticks of lollipops. But Colby shared with me the first student he hired made it for him and it was more sentimental than anything.

"Are you sure he can't take anything, Mr. Scott?" I whisper. "That pink stick was a gift to him. It wasn't purchased and I know he'd love to have it."

Mr. Scott is indecisive, and I know he's putting himself on the line to allow Colby to take anything, so he shocks me with his answer.

"Do you know for a fact no paper trail would lead to a purchase of it?"

"A hundred percent. A student made it for him and it was his very first employee." A milestone Colby was proud of. To give students a job for the summer was something he wanted to do.

Sure it helped him, but he knew it was hard to find jobs and it was a small thing he could do to help. His heart is one of the kindest ones I've ever known.

Mr. Scott nodded. "Let me think about it."

I can only nod and hope it turns into a positive for Colby tonight. When he enters his back room I follow him, leaving Mr. Scott in the front, speaking on his phone.

I find Colby sitting on his tiny worn loveseat in the dark.

"What can I do, Colbs?" Fuck, I don't like him like this. Colby isn't dark. He's all the light and joy you'd find in a kid's eyes in a candy store.

He barks a humorless laugh. "Find me a miracle to not lose my store. That would be a good start."

I ease myself next to him on the loveseat and the thrum of his tension is palpable.

"I'll do whatever I can for you that's within my power, you know that. I don't know how yet, but we're going to get you back operating this store as soon as possible. It's your dream and I won't sit by and watch you lose it. I'll help you rebuild it." Uncurling his fist from his thigh, I bring his hand to my mouth and kiss his knuckles. "From every ending, there's a new beginning."

He softens and leans into me. "Since when did you become so introspective and deep?"

"Since I went through hell to get back to you and have my own second chance. I never gave up, Colby, and neither should you." Grasping his chin between my finger and thumb, I turn him towards me. "He's just not gonna win, okay? It's a setback and we're going to restart. Have faith we can do this together."

He's silent for a long time. The low voice of Mr. Scott still speaking on his phone floats back and Colby finally leaves his anger and takes the nugget of hope I've presented.

"You're right. I already paid his stupid loan and told him to fuck himself once today. I'll get the final fuck you and have a bigger and better place."

"Damn right you will."

Mr. Scott knocks at the doorway and we both stand.

"Colby, do you have any personal effects you want to take home?"

"I have some meds and food in here I'd like to take for sure. I'll need my schedule so I can call my employees, too."

"That's fine. Do you need help packing anything?"

He shakes his head. "It's not much and won't take long."

He has an empty box nearby and places the few things from his mini fridge inside it along with the two bottles of pills from the shelf with his granola bars. He hesitates and then takes the fluffy blanket off the end of the loveseat too.

Satisfied there's nothing else he carries the box to the front and adds his scheduling book to the pile.

"I guess that's it."

I cast a glance at Mr. Scott and he motions towards the lollipop stand. "Hey, we can take one more thing." I pluck the lollipops off and pick up the stand with a smile. "I asked if we could."

"Is it going to get you in trouble, Mr. Scott?" Colby asks.

"No, I've documented it just in case. Dante said it was a gift, and if that's true it belongs to you."

Colby only nods and the three of us leave together. When Colby turns the key and the deadbolt clacks closed for the last time he remains at the door for a few moments before joining us.

When he does, he's not the sad Colby. He's the determined Colby and I know he's going to be okay.

"Hey Dante!"

I turn from my barn mucking to find Dan grinning and heading my way. The always casual and smiling cowboy, Dan. With his thumbs tucked into his belt loops he stands at the barn door waiting for me.

"Hey, is the new llama here? Mittens and I are ready!"

Since Mittens finally started eating she's been, well, she's been a llama. No more weird cat behaviour and for that I'm thankful. I'm no llama whisperer by any means, but I'll take the win. But Dan did say llamas should be kept in pairs or multiples for company and now that Mittens knows who she is, he wants her to have a friend.

"Heh, yeah, about that... " He rubs his hand behind his neck and I laugh.

"What did you do?"

"So I planned to just bring back the one, right? But when I get there the lady says there's still two left needing homes."

I smile. Classic Dan taking in everything he can. Including me. Even though it may add to my work load, I'm not complaining.

"And you brought back all three, I assume?"

"Well, one was really attached to the llama I committed to so I didn't want to break them up. And I wasn't going to leave the third one there all alone. That's just mean."

"I'll agree with you there." I wipe the sweat off my forehead and lean the shovel against the wall. Dan already has the trailer backed up to the barn doors. "Do you have a plan?"

"Open the trailer and let them out." He shrugs and I laugh again. Sometimes I wonder if he thinks anything through before doing it. Then I remember he does indeed think things through since he sat me down this morning with Blaze and Martin and asked for my input on what they planned to do to help Colby and me. There was so much thought put into that conversation it made my heart hurt.

"Let's let them walk right through to the pasture, then. Mittens is already out there."

This llama unloading goes much smoother than the last time. Three llamas exit the trailer with cautious steps. One's all black, there's one that's white with black spots and the third one is... different. The first two strutted through the barn and out to pasture like they've lived here their whole life.

When the third one stops at the edge of the barn and I get a good look at it, I raise an eyebrow at Dan.

"What?"

I sigh. "Dan, what the hell is wrong with this one?"

This llama takes two steps then looks around and then takes a hopping step before again taking another small step. I don't think this llama has any kind of problem I can help with.

"She's just different." He holds out his hand and the llama pokes its head towards it, but it misses. It's six inches to the left of where Dan holds his hand. "She's cross eyed and has no depth perception. But she's really sweet." The llama finally finds Dan's hand and is quite happy with the ear scratches he gives. When she's had enough, she continues her eclectic march through the barn and out to the pasture without misjudging the doorway. Although she does come close to bonking her head at the end but misses. She's also white and smaller than the others which I might safely assume is because the others eat faster than her and she misses the trough too much.

"I'll make sure she gets fed treats separately and doesn't miss out."

"Her name's Hawkeye."

I snort. "For real? A llama with vision issues is named Hawkeye?"

"The black one is Radar and the other one is Klinger. Hawkeye had her name before she was born. It just worked out that way."

"The owner was a fan of the show M.A.S.H., I guess?"

Dan chuckles. "His grandfather was, and he did it to humour the granddad before he died. Besides, everyone had a crush on Alan Alda then, so why not?" Dan turns serious and faces me. "Listen, we were all serious with the plan we put together to help you and

Colby. I know it's only been a short time, but how is he handling it all? No bullshit."

I puff a breath out and think of the best way to answer that. He's not okay, but he's coping well. Very well, but it's not something that will just be better overnight.

"At first he was moping. But now he's in full on stick it to the man mode. To be honest, I'm concerned with how hard he's thrown himself back into working at the brewery. It seems like I've barely seen him the last few days. He's gone from one extreme to the next, but I know he wants nothing more than to get the doors back open and have his business back."

"Martin told me he's been at Tilt-a-Whirl almost twenty-four hours a day since he went back. Sounds like we need an intervention."

"You know what? Let me talk to him tonight and if you don't mind, I'd like to ask for tomorrow afternoon off. He needs to get on Babe and get back to his happy place. Then you could lay out the plan to him."

He nods in agreement. "We can do that. Have him at the house tomorrow night and I'll make sure Blaze and Martin know."

Dan retreats and I stare out into the field of four llamas getting to know each other. Well, Mittens welcoming her new friends, at least. They seem to be completely at ease with each other and my imagination runs away with me, making up conversations they might be having. Hawkeye isn't left out and they move together as a unit with Mittens leading the way.

It's a lot like Dan and all us crew at the Ranch. Every time a new person gets added, the rest of the crew just seem to take us in and show us the way. There's no side eye or misplaced trust and jealousy. It's just someone else to help.

Colby may not be a paid member of this ranch, but he's respected and loved just the same. These men come together for animals, but their love and generosity goes way beyond that. They've given me another family and I'm damn fortunate to have a second chance at a life because of them.

It's time Colby learned the depths these people are willing to go to help him out.

Chapter 25

Colby

I forgot how much physical labour was involved when working at the brewery. Placing the last case of twenty-four cans into the back of the delivery van, I only pause for a minute to catch my breath. I'm not opposed to the labour, I'm just not used to it anymore. Lugging boxes of candy onto a counter a few times a week doesn't compare to loading a van with cases of beer every day.

"Hey Colby, you done loading?"

Zane, my boss and one of the owners here as well as a friend of the ranch, takes the clipboard from me with all the delivery info.

"I am. I'm just going to refill my coffee mug, hit the bathroom and then I'll start on making deliveries."

Zane smiles back and keeps the clipboard next to his chest. "No you're not."

"Oh, you need me to do something else then?"

"Yes! I need you to take the afternoon off." Zane checks the ignition of the van and pockets the keys before once again flashing a smile my way.

"But why? Those deliveries need to be made today and then you have to get that batch of IPA canned for the restaurants that ordered and were missed the last time. And then I need —"

"Colby, what you need to do is go home and come back tomorrow. You've been here for almost twenty-four hours a day all week. I don't mind paying you and I appreciate the work you do here, but you need to slow down." He places a hand on my shoulder with a gentle squeeze. "I know you want to get Lick it Up back open as soon as possible and I promise we're here to help you do that. But I won't let you burn yourself out before you even get that far."

Without me noticing, he's already steered me to the door and we're walking to my car. "When's the last time you went for a ride with Babe? Or spent quality time with Dante? It's not good to focus all your energy on one thing like this. You need some balance and you need to live."

He opens my car for me and in the way only Zane can, he makes me feel like I'm doing him a favour, and not the other way around.

Once I'm seated behind the wheel he gives me a thumbs up with a cheesy grin. "See you tomorrow and not until noon!"

He does have a point, though. I shift my car into drive and point myself towards home. Ever since Dante gave me that pep talk and I had to walk away from my shop, I've been hell bent to do whatever I could to get it back open. That included working eighteen-hour days, and I hadn't thought about the rest of my life taking a back seat while I did it.

Dante hasn't said anything either. His early mornings at the ranch have him out of the house before me and sometimes I don't even see him until one of us slides under the covers at night to join whoever went to bed first. I haven't been fair to him.

Zane's right, I need to be better at balancing things. I've spent five years hoping to have Dante back and now that he's here, we've had one thing after another come up and we still haven't had the quality time I've dreamed of.

When I arrive at my place, Dante's car is in the driveway already and I laugh to myself. I think my boss may have been part of a conspiracy for us to spend time together. With a pep in my step, I jog up the porch and let myself into the house.

"Hey, D! You home?"

Dante's head pokes around from the kitchen, and that smile of his could light the neighbourhood on the darkest of nights.

"I am." He wipes his hand on a dish towel and greets me at the door with a kiss so hot it could melt the vinyl siding.

"Wow. Can I get greeted like that every time I come home?"

He chuckles, and I trail after him into the kitchen.

"You can if we can arrange it so we're both home close to the same time."

I notice all the containers along the counter and raise an eyebrow. "What's all this?"

He playfully smacks my hand when I try to steal a grape.

"It's for our date."

The biggest, goofiest smile fills my face. "We're going on a date?"

"Yep. I've never taken you on a date and I've wanted to take you on one since forever. I've got plans, but you need to get ready."

"Well, what am I getting ready for?"

Taking me in his arms, he kisses my forehead. "An afternoon with your favourite guy and your favourite horse. That's all I'm going to tell you."

"Hmm, sounds amazing." I place a kiss on his lips that turns to more. My hands can't keep away from his body and one kiss just isn't enough. He gently pushes me away when I've backed him against the counter and I'm shamelessly rubbing myself on his leg.

"Save it for later, Colbs. I have a surprise planned for you." He cups the back of my head and drops a gentle kiss to my nose. "I'll finish this, you go change for a ride."

I fake moan in frustration. "Doesn't the song say save a horse and ride a cowboy? We could just skip the horse part and make our own ride." I wiggle my eyebrows and he laughs.

"Do as you're told and let me do this for you."

With another quick kiss, I back out of the kitchen, my mood boosted with our playfulness. I love this man to the depths of the ocean. If he wants to do something for me, I'm going to let him do it.

With a mock salute I head to our bedroom with his laughter sounding behind me.

I'm so happy I let Dante carry on with his plan. Being on my horse and out in the fresh air with the loves of my life is just what I need. The spring has truly sprung and we're heading into warmer summer nights. It's one of my most favourite times of the year. It's still chilly enough in the evening to need a sweater, but the days are warmer. The butterflies float about and the songbirds never seem to stop singing.

Being out in nature while watching Dante's broad back in front of me on one of the ranch's trail horses sets my soul on fire. Babe and her sure-footed walk along the path is the only thing keeping me grounded in the here and now. The squeak and sway of the saddle are just enough to keep from slipping away in a daydream. A daydream that couldn't possibly be better than my current reality.

So much has changed in a short time and through it all, I stopped focusing on the man in front of me. Yet he stuck by me, even when his price was much higher than mine. I only lost my store and he lost years of his life in prison. Years that he gave up for me. I don't know how I can ever love him back as much as he loves me.

But Zane was right and I'm going to try for better balance, because what good is a successful business or any other accomplishment without that one person to share it with? The one to cry with, laugh with, who will do anything to make you smile and lift your troubles.

We're drawing close to the end of the narrow part of the trail where it widens for us to ride side by side. He waits for Babe and I to catch up and no words are needed as his shy smile and the tip of his cowboy hat makes my knees weak. Thank god I'm already sitting.

I could be angry for losing the last five years with him, but I think I'm going to choose to enjoy him now instead, and be thankful for this chance.

The trail opens to the same meadow we were at last time and I'm puzzled as to why there's a tent set up near the tiny creek.

"I wonder if Dan knows people have set up camp on his property? Think we should see if they're around?"

At first he says nothing and I'm about to ask again, but he replies. "Dan knows. I asked him to set it up for me."

"Oh? Why?"

He shakes his head with a small smile. "You'll see."

Now more puzzled than before, we reach the tent and dismount, letting the horses drink before tying them nearby. Dante removes the saddle bags he packed and drops them at the front of the tent before turning to me with an outstretched hand.

Placing my hand in his, he kisses my knuckles and peers up at me from under his beautiful, long eyelashes.

"Colby," his hoarse voice, thick with emotion, draws a gasp from me. "When we made our plans all those years ago, one thing you always talked about was wanting to be in a field in a tent, gazing up at stars with the person you loved." He tosses his hat to the side and pulls me closer. "I hoped to make it happen one day when I knew I was your person." A brush of his thumb across my cheek. "It's not much of a date, there's no big dinners or fancy clothes. But it's a tent and I give you the only thing I really have left."

He pauses again to kiss me so gentle and sweet, I feel like I'm the most beautiful piece of treasure. But I also feel like I might crumble to my knees.

"You have all of me, Colbs. My heart you've had this whole time, but you can have the rest of me, too."

"D... you trying to make me cry or something?" I kid, but I cup his face with my shaking hands and press a kiss to his lips.

"No, I just want you to make me yours." He laughs softly and his breath tickles my neck. "I want my first time to be with you how you imagined. I want this to be the start of something new for us that never ends. I want it to be unforgettable."

"It doesn't matter where we are or what we do, it's going to be unforgettable because it's you, D."

No kiss from Dante has ever tasted so sweet. Nipping at my jaw, he places kisses wherever he can. Part of me wants to make a joke about not going all the way on our first date, but in a way, we've been dating our whole life. I'm lost to him completely. He's unbuttoning clothes, drawing me towards the tent without me even knowing what he's doing. He pauses his kisses and removes his shirt before going for mine and tosses them on the ground before opening the tent zipper.

"Come on in."

He holds it open for me and I kick off my boots to crawl inside. It's just a tiny two person tent with a mattress that fills the whole floor. There's at least six pillows and two sleeping bags spread out. There's a skylight and if it was night time I'd be able to do exactly as I always wanted and gaze up at the stars while in my lover's arms amidst the nature I love. It's so fucking perfect and so damn romantic I want to bawl like a baby over the fact he remembered after all this time.

He joins me, naked chest and messy hair with his jeans half open. The outline of his hard cock unmistakable in his pants. Pushing him down on his back, my hands roam his body and I'm delighted to see him shiver with every touch.

He lifts his hips and I tug his jeans all the way down and off with his boxers. It's not like we haven't been together sexually since he's been back. We've just never been like this. After he told me he's never been with anyone and we had our conversation about sex out here, that was when my mom showed up and ruined what I hoped would have been a passionate night. Our first time.

This is much better.

Sitting back on my heels, I drink in the sight before me. Dante naked with his legs spread and his cock leaving a smear on the fine hair on his stomach. His skin is already flushed pink from me watching him and his chest rises and falls with his shallow breaths. I scramble in the small space to lose the rest of my clothes and prowl over top of him. Our too warm bodies press together and a contented sigh crosses my lips.

"I'll never get tired of feeling your skin next to mine." I push myself up on my elbows to kiss his collarbone. "I don't think I'll ever get used to being with you like this." I trail kisses down his chest and revel in the taste of his skin on my lips. Dante's sweet sighs fill the small tent and my heart feels like it might just bust out of my chest like the Kool Aid man.

I kiss my way back up to his neck as I brush our hard dicks together and whisper, "Please tell me in all your planning you have lube here."

"It's in one of the saddlebags with... other stuff." He breathes.

"Sounds mysterious."

I spin around to open the tent and pull the bags in along with our discarded shirts. The first bag has the snacks he packed and my heart pitter patters again when I notice he has a Fun Dip packed in there. Can he get anymore fucking fuzzy and romantic? My hands scramble to open the second one and when I do, a loan groan escapes me when I see what he brought with him.

Holding up the bright orange silicone plug, I turn to find Dante with hooded eyes licking his lips.

"You want me to use this on you, D?"

He gulps, "If-f-f, you want to. I tried it a few times already." My eyebrows shoot up with his admission. "I liked it, but I don't know if... I don't know if you need it to, um, like.... "

His words trail off as he bites his lip and looks away. Seriously, he's too damn cute when he's all shy with me, and this is what I get to have for the rest of my life.

"You don't know if I need it before I use my dick on you?"

He narrows his eyes. "I was trying to not ruin the moment, Colby," he huffs. "But yes, I didn't know what you liked."

I take what I want out of the bag and place it next to his hip before blanketing my body over his again. "I like you." His skin burns molten hot under my touch and I work to keep my lust in check. To be his first partner, the only one to be inside his body, stops my breath. He truly is giving me everything he has. "No, that's not right. I love you, and you're nervous, but so am I."

He pulls my face down to his to kiss me, but keeps our foreheads connected. "Why are you nervous?" he pants.

"Because I don't want to do anything you don't like and... well, I'm afraid it might be over too fast because this is a dream I never thought would come true."

And there's the big, enormous thing that you're offering me your body to me like this. It makes me hyperventilate.

"Just make me feel good."

With that instruction, I proceed to do just that. I kiss and tease my way down to his throbbing cock and I don't take him down right away. Instead I tease him with my tongue and lap at the constant leak from his tip. There's not a lot of room in this tent, maybe the dream would have worked better when we were teenagers, but I've maneuvered us both into a comfortable position so I can work him open properly. Which I don't want to do with his hunter orange plug. We're going to have to talk about not buying hideous coloured sex toys. I'm doing it with my tongue and fingers because I want to be in touch with him at all times. Me and only me.

Dante graduates from sweet sighs to low moans and when he pushes back on my fingers I take his dick back into my mouth.

"Oh my god. Colbs... feels so good. Fuck... "

I moan around his dick, because he's right. Nothing has ever felt like this and I want it to be like this forever. I work in another finger and his body stiffens.

"You gotta breathe, D. Relax, baby."

He listens and breathes as I've said, his eyes wide as he peers down at me between his thighs.

I need to kiss him while we do this. I don't feel like I'm connected to him, like I'm missing out on his reactions. Removing my fingers, I reposition us on our sides so I can watch his face and swallow his moans.

"Colby... " He breathes with a shudder and drops his head to my shoulder.

"I know, D. I know."

With a soft hand, I spread him underneath me and grab the lube bottle to slick myself up. I move as slow as a turtle through molasses, letting him adjust with each small advancement until I'm finally only half way in. A light sweat breaks on his forehead and I lean down to kiss his dry lips, running my tongue along them for him until he swallows and pushes his hips up to take more of me.

We both moan and Dante pulls me down to him again, kissing me with so much pent up desire my head swims.

Finally buried in him, I drop myself to my forearms and he wraps his legs around me with the first small thrust.

His fingers clutch at my back and I bury my face in his neck, kissing his ear.

"Fuck, D. You feel so good. I can't believe we're doing this finally."

"I've missed you so much."

He tugs at my hair and I lift my head to stare into the brown eyes that see all the way to my soul. This is where I belong.

Our slick bodies rock together and low moans fill the air until his body starts to shake around me. "You gonna come, D?"

The warm fluid on my stomach with his strangled moan answers my question. Feeling my own balls draw up, I pull out to finish on him, mixing my load with his.

I do believe I just went to heaven.

"Is it always going to feel like this?" he pants, as his shaky hand reaches up to my face.

"I think as long as it's me and you it will always be like this." I rummage in the stuff he brought to find the wet wipes and towel to clean up with. "You're gonna be a little sore," I murmur when I clean him up.

"Worth it. A thousand times worth it."

Settling next to him, we lay together, caressing and sharing kisses filled with the promise of a future and a love so big, it barely fits in my heart.

There's no stars to stare up at, but that's okay. I'd rather stare at the man in my arms and be thankful he made his way back to me.

Chapter 26

Colby

Dante and I drifted off for a while after our emotionally charged sex. The intensity of our feelings as well as the physical exertion was enough for me to float away into the most peaceful of sleeps. One we both needed, if his gentle snores are any indication.

I poked my head out the tent flap earlier to make sure the horses were still okay, which they were. I even pulled on my boxers and snuck over to the creek to wash up a little. Dante had the foresight to pack a bar of soap. Whether he wanted it for post sex clean up or something else, it sure came in handy.

Dante stirs against me and he blinks open his sleepy eyes just as my stomach rumbles.

"Hey, handsome. Your stomach sure is loud." He tilts his face up and I place a kiss on his sweet lips.

"Sorry, but we should probably eat and head back soon. It still gets dark early."

He stretches and sits up searching for clothes and he smiles when he notices the folded pile I placed in the corner.

"Let me just run over to the creek real quick to wash."

After Dante flashes me his ass while he stumbles trying to put his boxers on, I start unpacking the food he chose for us. I get all mushy inside when I notice it's all my favourites. There's green grapes, cheese crackers, slices of kielbasa and little cubes of mozzarella cheese. He even packed adorable napkins with moose on them.

Dante shimmies back into the tent and carefully sits across from me and the tiny picnic.

"You brought all my faves. I love it."

He pops a cheese cube in his mouth with a grin. "That's what you're supposed to do on a date isn't it? Impress your date and make them feel special?"

"Yes, but you know you don't have to impress me. Ever."

"I want to make you feel special, though. Every day, not just on a date." He puffs out a breath and looks so damn shy and cute I still see the awkward nineteen-year-old boy who drew hearts in the sand for me. I reach my hand behind his head and pull him close to me.

"You do make me feel special. You always have. You don't need to try to make up the last five years for me, D." Leaning in, I brush my lips over his. "Let's just have a new beginning, starting now."

With renewed confidence he kisses me back and forces a grape in my mouth with a chuckle.

"So, you were right about us needing to get back." He feeds me another grape and this time I don't fight him. I won't complain if the most amazing, sweet man ever wants to force food down my throat. Nor will I ever forget this experience. I always knew Dante had a more sweet than salty side, and I'm so damn fortunate to be the one on the receiving end of it.

"Why? Do you have more surprises for me?"

"Well... not me personally, but Dan does."

"Dan has a surprise for me?"

"There's a lot of people on the ranch who want to help you with the store. It's my understanding they have a proposal to present to you."

This isn't what I thought he'd say and I'm not sure how I feel about it. But his hand on my knee draws my focus back to him.

"Colby, if there's one thing I've learned the last few months, it's to accept help when offered. There's no shame in accepting it and it doesn't make you any less of a business owner or person. In fact, it makes you stronger." He passes my shirt over to me and tugs his own on. "People who help people are the best thing to have on your side. I hope you see that."

I've been so used to being on my own and doing it all my way and in my time, I failed to understand this simple message. Dan came through for me with Babe several years ago. While I worked hard to try to pay him back as much as I could with labour or little things for the animals, I overlooked one simple thing. He's just a kind person who wants to help and expects nothing in return.

When I accepted Dan's help then, it was with relief, because Babe was not at fault. She was a horse needing a home and he gave her one. While I wished I didn't need his help, I still took it. But at some point in the last few years, I've not been able to accept that same unconditional offer of help in any other area of my life. I refused my mom's offer of financial help and I was determined to do it all myself. Right down to not letting Landon help me with the set up and building of all my store displays.

"Hey, you okay?" Dante's kind eyes watch me closely and I feel like such an ass. He slept in his car and accepted help from strangers to feed and clothe him without letting his pride get in the way. He found a job, made friends and found his way back to me. All with help from others.

"I'm an idiot," I croak.

He brushes my cheek with the back of his hand. "But you're my idiot, and I love you anyway."

I snort and steal another kiss. "Lets get packed up and back to the ranch, then. This idiot could've screwed up his life if it weren't for you."

"Colbs, there's nothing that can't be fixed with the help of good friends."

We left the tent behind and packed up our things on Dante's horse, Charlie, the same as how we arrived. We take the trail back to the ranch with me behind Dante, and I notice how much he keeps shifting in his saddle. When we get home I'll make sure he has an epsom salt bath.

The ranch yard is bustling with activity when we arrive as evening chores are carried out and other people with animals boarding here spend time with them. It's still early evening but it feels like midnight. I'm exhausted, but in the best possible way. After checking all the horses are in for the night and taken care of, hand in hand we head up to Dan's house. Before we can knock, the door swings open and I'm met with a smiling Blaze.

"Ah, here he is. Did you two have a nice date?"

I look at Dante, who ducks his head with a grin, and my neck heats. Good to know the whole ranch knows what we were up to out there.

"It was fantastic. I didn't know he was such a romantic." I kiss Dante's cheek and there's a loud aww from the dining room. Dan and Martin smile like proud parents and I shake my head.

"Well get in here, love birds, we have much to discuss." Blaze pushes us into the farm house and closes the door while Dan motions for us to sit at the dining room table.

"Can I get you two anything? Coffee, beer, water?" Martin stands at the fridge waiting as we pull out chairs.

"I'd love some water," I say.

"Me too, Martin," Dante agrees and Martin pours us each a glass from the Brita in the fridge before joining us.

Dan pulls out the chair next to him for Martin and his tender gaze for him warms my heart. I know them both, but I've never seen them interact on a couple level so intimately. Blaze sits at one end of the table, hands clasped in front of him and dressed in the familiar jeans and t-shirt attire. No perfectly styled hair today, either. His black Stetson has been in place all day and now rests on the table next to him.

"As you know, we're aware of what happened with you both and we want to extend our sympathy to you. Life is hard enough, but to find out your father and stepfather played a part in destroying your life, that has to be hard to accept," Blaze says.

"I've had a few years more than Colby to accept that part," Dante says. "But you're right, it's not easy."

"I know if we ever lost the brewery in any kind of situation, I'd be crushed. All my partners would be." Martin reaches over to squeeze my shoulder. "Which is why it's been a topic of discussion with us and Dan the past few days."

Blaze clears his throat. "We took care of the most pressing matter of your loan. Which in retrospect may not have been needed, but I know that part was important to you."

"And I can't thank you enough for that. I think it helped with closure on the whole situation."

"Colby, you've been coming here for almost five years now? It's been awhile." Dan smiles fondly my way and I return the same affection.

"It has been. I'm so grateful you helped me keep Babe. I would've had to sell her if you didn't offer the arrangement you did."

"If you ask Blaze, I'm quite good at offering arrangements."

Blaze's laughter booms out. "You're smooth, I'll give you that. Pretty sure Martin can back that up."

Martin laughs and turns his gaze to Dan. "He talked a city boy who hates mud and dirt into living on a ranch part time and keeping a cow in the living room. I'd say he's as smooth as silk."

Dan drops a kiss on Martin's cheek. "And I regret nothing."

"Anyway, Colby, " Dan continues, "I'm sure you and Dante would like to get on with your evening. So we'll get to the point."

"With the loss of your building, you need a place for Lick it Up 2.0 and that's where I come in." Martin smiles, eager to be involved. "As you know already from your employment with us Colby, we share a space downtown with the Crumb and Cake bakery. You've met Parker before, I believe."

"Oh I have! He's the guy who always sings at the coffee house and makes those amazing chocolate chip cookies, right?"

"Same guy, yep." Martin chuckles. "He does make a mean cookie. We shared the space with him when he first opened because we partnered with him on events. It worked well for people planning parties and weddings to order their cake and beer in the same place. Now that the brewery is established and we have consistent orders, we don't need to maintain such a large retail space in town." He reaches across the table to drag a file folder over. Flipping through it, he removes a page and passes it to me.

"The details are there for you to take home and think about. But Tilt-a-Whirl would like to give that space over to you as soon as you want it. Parker will now keep a limited display on our behalf in his shop and direct any inquiries to us. The other business we used to generate from that location was completely seasonal and we can make that up if we want to by attending seasonal markets, but it's not affecting our bottom line to be of any detriment to us."

I skim the paper and notice the rent amount. "This rent is far too low. I can't accept that."

It's an instant reaction to say no. I can't help it.

Dante whispers in my ear. "Remember the help of good friends, Colbs."

Martin chuckles. "With new debt and establishing a new location, your costs will be higher than you're used to. For six months your rent will either be $200/m or a percentage of your sales. Whatever is less, not more. After that we'll revisit and negotiate something more inline with what you'd expect from a commercial lease. This is how Tilt-a-Whirl, me, Dylan, Matts and Zane, want to help."

I can only stare at the paper in front of me and feel the flutter of hope. A new location as soon as I say the word. I didn't expect this when I woke up today and it's a huge lift to my plan.

Dan claps his hands together, his eyes shining with excitement. "My turn!" I laugh and Dante squeezes my thigh under the table. I grasp his hand in return and accept his support. "The space the boys are giving you is down right naked. You need displays and shelving before you can open. I've had many of my crew in the workshop with River for the past week building some. River is a fucking talent with building and designing anything with wood, so you know they'll be quality and look gorgeous. Just say the word and we'll move them to the new space. He's even making a custom counter for you."

My eyes water and I can't find the words to voice any of the thoughts in my head right now. The amount of savings for new fixtures is staggering and because River can build beautiful things I'm doubly blessed. I don't know how to gracefully accept all this.

"I know it's a lot for you to take in, Colby, but you're a part of this ranch and we help our own." Blaze's voice draws my watery eyes to him and his gentle smile settles me. "I didn't know when I set off as a fresh graduate that I'd create something so massive I'd be a billionaire overnight. I didn't ask for that, but I got it. Just like you didn't ask for this situation, to lose what you worked so hard at literally overnight." He pauses and Dan slides the folder his way. Blaze picks out not a sheet, but an envelope and hands it to me.

"All the details are in there and I'd like you to review it together tonight. I've put my cell phone in there too so you can call me with questions. If you accept it, just sign it and bring it back to me."

"I also have one final thing," Martin pipes up. "Marketing and design is what I do best and I know you'll need a new sign. I've taken the liberty to design a few new logos and signage mockups for you. You'd just have to take it to the vendor of your choice to have new signs made. Or not use them at all, but since you're in a new location with a new feel, I think a fresh new logo would help. Even if you don't like what I've done we can work together until we get it right."

"Thank you and I think that's a great idea. I'd love to see what you came up with." I gulp from the water glass and stomp down all the sappy shit I want to spew out at these people. No, not people. My friends. My extended family who I'm incredibly blessed to have, but I'm drowning with all the unsolicited support.

"I'll look these things over tonight and get back to you." Inhaling a deep, calming breath I continue. "It's a lot for me to digest right now, but please know I'm beyond grateful."

"Take your time. We're not going anywhere and call if you have questions." Blaze stands as Dante and I do. "I still want that Tiger Tail ice cream."

I manage a soft laugh.

"I'll take him home. Thank you so much, I know Colby is having a hard time with words right now, but I appreciate what you're all doing."

"Always our pleasure. See you in the morning, Dante."

Dan leads us to the door and once we're out in the farmyard and away from the amazing generous men I'm fortunate enough to call friends, I hold onto Dante tight.

With all the incredible news, he's the only thing that feels real right now. And I need to wrap my head around the fact I can have a store much sooner than I expected.

As long as I accept the help from my friends.

Chapter 27

Dante

The drive home is quiet as Colby clutches the envelope and paper in his hands. Two small items that have the power to change his life. I just hope he accepts it and realizes that even if it was charity, there's a million ways he could pay it back to someone else in the future. I won't forget the woman, Molly, at the second hand store who put clothes on my back and pointed me to Dan. Sometime in the future I'll also repay Dan's kindness to me to someone else.

It's just what you need to do. If everyone could be kind, the world would be a much better place.

My poor Colby is so sweet and used to being the one helping. He doesn't know how to accept the offer of help for himself. The headlights bounce off the front of the house when I pull in and I turn to him when he doesn't open the door right away.

"Hey, I know you've got a lot going through your head right now. Let's go in and talk, okay?"

He nods in agreement and together we climb the front steps and enter the quiet space. Landon left a note on the counter that he won't be home tonight, which is sweet of him. Colby drops to the sofa after kicking off his shoes and gently opens the envelope from Blaze. When he brings his hand to cover his mouth I know it's something huge.

Inhaling a breath, he meets my eyes. "Blaze has, ah, he... he's offering me an interest free loan for inventory and... " Colby shakes his head. "And he wants to gift me the funds for the ice cream expansion in exchange for me offering free ice cream to kids twice a summer or more frequently if I want."

"That's amazing, Colby. Blaze is a nice guy and he'd not want to make any money off that loan. He's a businessman, sure, but he's more of a philanthropist than anything, I think."

"Maybe that's why he keeps his identity a secret. He wants to pick and choose who he helps instead of being approached by just anyone."

"It could be, I can see that. But you know he's not doing it just to be kind, right? He's doing it because you're a friend to everyone you meet, Colbs. And if I had to guess, it's also his way of trying to right some wrongs that were done to you."

Colby is silent for so long I think he needs time alone to think. But when I stand, he asks me to sit back down.

"These guys are all giving me a lot. Free fixtures, free graphic design, rent that's practically nonexistent and an interest free loan. Not to mention my expansion cost for an ice cream stand that's probably going to cost more now since the location is different. I'll have to start getting estimates again and pricing equipment for a different space. It seems like too much, like how is it possible I can find all that from one group of people?"

Taking his hand, I kiss his palm and study the conflict on his handsome face. He wants to say yes so badly, but something still holds him back.

"Sometimes good luck happens to people, and sometimes bad luck happens to people. But in the end, no matter what kind of luck it is, it's still yours. So you do with it as you see fit. It's yours and only yours, Colby."

Remaining quiet, he flips the business card in his fingers with Blaze's information on it.

"I can't tell you what to do. It's your decision. But you've been given a second chance, Colbs, and that's fucking amazing. Not everyone gets that opportunity." I stand again and he peers up at me. "I'm going to have a shower. Why don't you call him and join me when you're done."

"You should have a bath, you're sore and Landon keeps salts under the sink. I wanted to run you a bath."

That's Colby. Would rather help someone else, no matter how small. Just like when I fell once when we were on a hike and my hand was gushing blood. He tripped on his way to help me and ignored his own wounds until I was okay.

"Okay. I'll shower then run a bath and I hope you come join me after you've talked to Blaze. That's my compromise."

Not giving him any chance to keep second guessing his choice, I saunter down the hall removing my clothes as I go. Tossing them in the laundry basket, I walk naked to the bathroom since Landon isn't home, and start the shower. I even find the salts Colby was talking about and I may just do the soak thing after all. That horse ride back was a smidge uncomfortable, so maybe I should take my boyfriend's advice.

Although I kind of like the twinges I keep feeling because I remember why I ache and then I get to relive the amazing afternoon we had.

With my shower done and still no sign of Colby, I switch to running the bath, and as my hand reaches for the tub of epsom salt, Colby's hand covers mine.

"How long have you been standing there?"

"Long enough to track that bead of water that ran from your shoulder down your back and onto your ass."

He nudges me and takes the container of salts. "I want to do this for you."

I step out the way, naked and dripping on the bath mat and watch Colby as he shakes in salt and then reaches into the tub to test the temperature and swirl the salts around. He rips off his t-shirt before reaching in to swirl the water around more and it's then I notice the change.

His shoulders are relaxed and even his arms flex with ease, the tension all but disappeared and replaced with a quiet confidence. The pride blooming in me can't be contained and a smile fills my face.

"You can get in now, D." He smiles back. "What are you looking at me like that for?"

"No reason."

I make a show of sliding my warm wet body up against his still dry one and he laughs. An amazing sound that I wish I could bottle and listen to forever.

Easing myself into the water, I lean back and find him watching me with the goofiest grin. He starts to peel his jeans off and motions for me to sit up.

"You think you're going to fit in here with me?"

"Remember what you said earlier about luck? And that you should just accept whatever you're given because it's yours?"

"I do."

The boyish grin I fell in love with more than five years ago graces his handsome face and for a moment I'm speechless.

"Well it's your good luck I'm getting in the tub with you, so you should accept it because I'm yours." He eases behind me and we jostle in the tiny tub. Two large guys shouldn't be in a tub this size together, but I'm not complaining. We both laugh when water splashes out onto the floor.

But I lean back into him and nothing has ever felt so perfect in my life.

"You'll help me scoop ice cream on the free days, right?"

I squeeze his hands he wrapped around me and tilt back for a kiss. "I'll scoop every day if you need me to and even the days you don't."

"D?"

"Yeah?"

"I'm really fucking lucky."

We sit in the tub until the water goes cold and even in the silence
I hear everything he's saying.

Chapter 28

Colby

4 months later

My fingers run across the smooth lacquered finish of my new countertop for Lick it Up 2.0. River has done an incredible job. He doesn't just build fine quality furniture, he's a top notch wood carver. No pun intended. The heavily glossed top is the practical work surface it needs to be, but it's the front panel of the counter that has me speechless.

An intricately carved name, Lick it Up is the primary focus. I'm no expert on the types of wood used for carving, but it looks expensive. Various wrapped candies, lollipops and ice cream cones all surround the name. Each one is just as intricately carved and painted as the name. The time he must have put into this for me is almost too much for me to handle.

"So what do you think? Blaze thinks I maybe overdid it, but I really liked carving all the little candies. And my dad did some of the painting." River hovers behind me, hands stuffed in his pockets. "He has to pass the time and wanted to help, I hope that's okay."

"It's more than okay," I croak. The sting behind my eyes comes fast and as much as I try to hide it, a grateful tear slips out. "It's beautiful and I can't thank you enough for this. It's far more than I ever dreamed."

And it really is. To properly compensate River for this I'd need several months of wages, easily. He did this, and all the other display pieces for my new store in the last four months. While this piece obviously took the most time to create – the other ranch hands took over the smaller pieces – River's care and obvious skill applied to this will take some time for me to process.

I should be used to it by now, but every time one of these guys does something else for me it overwhelms me all over again.

Tomorrow all the shelving gets delivered to my new space. Dante and I have spent the last two weeks at the store directing the sign installation and cleaning up after the contractor. We painted walls and received deliveries. Once these displays are in place tomorrow, we'll be unpacking and arranging and all the other last minute stuff. My original store has been gone for five months, but it's returning better than before. It will even be open in time for Christmas shoppers, my most profitable time of the year. A thought I couldn't even entertain a few months ago.

"I'm glad you like it. And for what it's worth, Colby, I was honoured to do this for you. We all need a break and I just love to carve. It was just as good for me as it was for you."

Blaze enters the workshop with a blast of chilly October air behind him, followed by Alec and Zane. Zane insisted he come over with snacks for everyone tonight even though the big move isn't until tomorrow.

"Hey guys." River waves a hello to the group that's both endearing and not necessary. "I was just telling Colby how this was such a fun thing for me to do. My dad is thrilled his painting will be in public." He chuckles and his fondness for his dad is evident.

Blaze smiles warmly at River and I don't miss the blush that creeps up River's cheeks.

"Which one did he do again, Riv?" Blaze squats down to inspect the carved pieces.

"He did the pink blow pop and all the little jelly beans." The pride in River's voice is unmistakable and I'll have to make a point of finding his dad to say a special thank you.

Zane settles a few bags on the makeshift table set up to the side. A leftover piece of plywood over a few sawhorses.

"I brought you some new cider I need sampled and some food to soak it up." Zane lines up a row of red plastic cups and produces a growler from one of his bags. "This is a hard apple cider I'm trying to perfect and serve in the brewery's restaurant for the fall. I need some opinions on it." He grimaces. "Since it's already fall."

"It's not pumpkin spice, is it?" Alec grumbles.

"I said apple. It's not pumpkin so calm down." Zane fills the cups and passes them around. He's particularly focused on Alec's reaction.

"Well, what do you think?" We all take time to taste the brew and I quite like it. It's like a tart apple juice, but it has a kick to it at the end I can't quite place.

"What kind of apples did you use?" Alec smells his cup like he's a cider sommelier.

"I used a granny smith primarily, but then I mixed it with the honey crisp apples we found at that apple farm to take down the tartness a bit." He drops his voice. "I know you prefer it on the sweeter side."

Alec nods and takes another gulp. "It's good, Zane. I like it."

"I do too. There's another taste in it I can't quite place, though. Apples and something else. It's really good."

The other guys all line up for a second cup and start picking at the snacks Zane brought. He's most likely trying out new recipes to use in the restaurant, just like the cider. He seems to always show up at Alec's with food samples, and Dante's brought home a few things before when Zane brings too much.

Blaze slides up next to me and bumps my shoulder. "Where's Dante?"

Ah, right. The whole reason why all my friends have come together to help me reopen my store, Dante's father and my stepfather. It's been a tough time waiting to hear what would happen to him, but we finally got word yesterday and he's been out of sorts with it.

"He's out with the llamas. We heard from the attorney yesterday."

Blaze's warm eyes fill with sympathy. "It's not good news?"

I puff out a shaky breath. "Some? I think Dante was hoping for more." I toss my cup into the garbage can. "I'm going to go check on him. If the guys need to leave before I'm back, can you tell them thanks and I'll see them tomorrow? I don't want to bring anymore attention to Dante if he's not ready."

Blaze nods and lowers his voice. "I get it. Slip out, don't worry. But if you need anything, call okay?" He squeezes my arm and with a nod I slip out the door and away from the somewhat celebratory mood in the workshop. The October air is icy and it feels like an early winter is on its way. The night has already fallen, but my path is lit with the moonlight across the farmyard and I slowly peek into the llama barn letting my eyes adjust to the soft glow of the barn's lights.

I can make out four llama bodies, but no Dante. If he's not here, there's only one other animal he'd be with.

Spinning on my heel, I jog over to the horse barn and walk quietly down to Babe's stall. My heart breaks in two with the scene before me. Dante must have skipped the llamas completely and come here first. Babe's mane has been braided like she's about to step into a show ring. He started braiding and weaving things as a way to calm his anxiety when he was in prison. Since he returned and moved in with me, we have several hand braided rugs and other items around the house. His creations have multiplied exponentially this week as we've waited to hear from Mr. Scott.

"Hey, D. You okay?" His forehead rests against Babe's neck and his arms are around her. Like she understands the need for calm and quiet, she greets me with a quiet snuffle instead of her usual snicker.

He turns his face to me and when I notice the puffy, red eyes, I draw him into my arms.

"Talk to me, D. I thought you were doing okay?"

He sighs against my chest. "I am. It's just... it just sort of hit me that it's over and I'm... I don't know."

Babe noses him and he digs out a sugar cube from his pocket. "Thanks for listening, Babe. You're such a good girl."

"I guess I was hoping more would happen to him? Is that bad?"

"No," I clip. "He forced you into running drugs, for fuck's sake. You were only nineteen. You went to prison for three years because of him. It's not bad to hope for him to suffer for what he did. He's not a nice man and you're human."

"I just keep thinking fifteen years in a minimum security prison isn't long enough. He shouldn't have a life to look forward to after his sentence. What about your mom? She lost the house because of him and lived in fear of her own life, Colbs."

"That's true, but she has a new place, remember? And she's safe." Mr. Scott stepped away from the case once his colleagues knew the evidence collected would stand. I was right, assuming there might be something between them. She just sent us an email with her new address, a house they share. Mom is picking up the pieces and moving forward just like we are.

Dante leaves Babe's stall and paces in the middle of the barn. Other horses poke their heads out of their stalls to watch him pulling at his hair as he lets it all out.

"What if you didn't know this crew at The Broken Horn, Colby? You'd have lost your store for good. You'd be back to doing three jobs and planning and saving all over again. And... and... what if you couldn't work and you couldn't pay rent? You might have lost Babe!"

I know he's just scared and maybe even a little guilty because it was his dad who caused all this mess to my mom and I. But I hate seeing him like this. As much as I'm still sometimes scared about the future, I need to be there and assure him there's nothing to worry about.

"But I didn't, D."

He stops pacing and steps up to me, cradling my face in his hands with a gentleness that takes my breath away.

"I almost lost you." He breathes against my lips. "I almost lost you forever because of him."

"But you didn't." I make sure my voice is strong. Because he did almost lose me forever and it's a place I never want to go back to. "You're here with me. It's all going to work out."

He closes his eyes and rests his forehead on mine. "How can you be so sure?"

"Because when I'm with you, there's no room for doubts."

"You make it sound so easy to forget."

I pull away to look into his warm brown eyes. "It's not that I forget, it's that I prefer to look ahead to the good stuff and that's you." Lacing my fingers into his I tug him towards the barn door. "I lived the same five years you did D. They weren't as hard as yours, but if there's one thing I learned through all this, it's to look ahead and not back."

He pauses in the barn aisle. "The bailiff let me see him. You know, before they sent him away." His throat works to make the words and stares off into the distance. "I don't know why I even wanted to see him after all this time, but I did."

Dante hadn't told me this before. I wish I had known so I could support him.

He exhales and returns his gaze to me. "I think I was hoping for... an apology? Or maybe just a sliver of something human from him." He looks away again and my heart shatters. He's too kind to be treated like this.

"What did he say?" I whisper, and grip his hand tighter.

His laugh is hollow. "That he's sorry he didn't have a better son."

"Oh, D.."

He shakes his head. "Let it go. I'm sorry I didn't have a better father, but at least I know he never saw me the way a real father should. It's time to move on and not look back, just like you said."

We stop at my car and glance over to the workshop, where the lights still shine and the guys' voices carry out into the night.

"Should we go say goodbye?"

"It's fine. Blaze knows where I went and we'll be back tomorrow morning for the move."

He squeezes my hand before he places a kiss on the back of it.

"Colbs?"

"Yeah?"

"Thanks for looking out for me."

"Always, D."

He peers up at the moon and the black sky before turning back to me. His eyes aren't so sad now and my heart lifts to see him accept it's time to move on and move forward. He's been through so much, we both have, but I know he'll be okay. I'll make sure of it.

The future starts now.

Dante's soft snores beside me bring me peace, but not enough for me to fall into the same slumber he has. Slipping out of bed, I pad to the kitchen for a snack and I hold in a yelp when I find Landon sitting in the dark living room already.

"You can't sleep either?" I whisper when he looks up from his book. The book light he uses has a bright yellow duck head for a lamp and it always makes me smile.

"No. I'm just nervous about my move." He laughs and sets the book down, but his pinched brow never wavers.

"Wanna talk about it?"

I think he will, but he shakes his head with a huff. "You have enough going on, Colby. Are you excited for tomorrow?"

"I am. And nervous too. It's like the first time all over again."

He chuckles. "First times are memorable, some good and some bad." Running his hand down his face, his boyish grin returns. "Remember the first time we went to a party at college and drank that vile purple juice?"

I groan at the not good memory. "Ugh, purple jesus. The most disgusting drink ever." We fight to keep our laughter down and not wake Dante. "It was even worse when it came back up later."

"But if you hadn't puked so hard to wake me up, I would never have known I liked to cuddle."

He winks at me and I drop my head in my hands. "I really thought you were into me, drunk or not. I was never so embarrassed when you peeled me off and said, *I don't do guys*."

We both giggle some more and even though Landon doesn't want to talk about his upcoming move, I know this is his way of telling me he's going to miss me. But I don't want to turn the giggles into sadness so I keep it light.

"I can't wait to visit you in New York. You'll take me to a hockey game, right? That's a job perk?"

"I hope so. I'd love to take you, but you might have to watch it yourself. I might have to be taking notes or something."

I raise my eyebrows. "Really? The strength and conditioning guys need to be that involved?"

He shrugs. "I'm not sure yet. But really, I'd love to have you visit. Dante too, if he can."

I yawn and pop the last grape from my snack in my mouth.

"You should get some sleep, Lan. You're gonna fucking kill this job, stop worrying."

He picks up his book again with a smile. "Thanks. Get back to sleeping beauty before he notices you're gone."

With a wave, I walk back to our room and sneak back in. Dante stirs when I slip back under the covers next to him and he slots himself against me in his sleep.

My life may have changed for the worse all those years ago, but now, it's only changing for the better.

Epilogue

Colby

The following June

"Shelby, wait, wait!"

With a sigh she spins around. "What now, Colby?"

"There's still Tiger Tail for Blaze right?"

"Yes, and you've asked that at least ten times already."

It's the first free ice cream day of the season. Lick it Up 2.0 was successfully open in time for the Christmas candy rush thanks to the marketing efforts of Martin, and me finally accepting help from friends. Now I'm in my first summer season at the new location and I'm fulfilling one of Blaze's conditions. It's the last day of school for kids and the schools announced free ice cream to the students a few days ago.

I've posted flyers all over town and even paid for a radio spot. I want to pay it forward, just like Dante's been teaching me.

I've ordered extra ice cream that my business neighbour Parker allowed me to store in his freezer, and I'm freaking out about possibly running out of ice cream. I've prepared all month for this and the stress of disappointing even one child weighs on me. I also don't want to let Blaze down.

"Head Scooper reporting for duty!"

Dante enters the store after changing and I burst out laughing.

"Where did you get that hat? And what's with all the pink?"

Dante stands before Shelby and me wearing one of those old school paper hats you'd see the men wearing at soda shops and the brightest bubblegum pink shirt I've ever seen. Or perhaps the shade is flamingo. Either way, it's so bright I should have sunglasses on.

"I ordered it online and I'll have you know I think I look amazing!"

He smooths his shirt, proud as a peacock, and I shake my head.

"You look something, alright," Shelby mutters and I snort.

"You're always amazing. Just make sure you scoop fast. I'll be watching the cone supply and running for more ice cream as needed."

The first group of kids arrive and it's instant pandelirium. Shouting voices asking for two flavours at once, is it true it's free, and did I know Batman was cooler than Spiderman? I didn't know, but I do now.

And still more kids come. And even more, and I've already run over to Parker's twice, and I'm starting to think I'll run out of ice cream. With ten minutes to spare before we close up, Blaze and River arrive and Blaze peers into my mostly empty ice cream case.

"How many buckets did you go through?" he asks.

"Eight, maybe nine? It's a lot. I only have one box of cones left too. So, easily two hundred kids came by, maybe more, because a few asked for bowls instead."

"Great! Is there any left for me?" I don't have the heart to tell him mostly what I have left is his flavour because only six people on the planet eat the stuff.

Dante serves him a Tiger Tail cone and River chooses butterscotch.

Shelby drifts off, cleaning up, and River helps Dante with bringing in the street signs, leaving Blaze and I alone.

"I'd say the first free ice cream day was a success. When do you plan the next one?"

"I think Labour Day weekend. The last hurrah before the kids go back, cheer them up before they lose their summer freedom."

Blaze chuckles and licks at his ice cream cone. "Summer freedom was always the best for the ones who had it."

"How come free ice cream is so important to you, Blaze? Can I ask that?"

He takes a moment and nods with a far away expression on his face.

"I grew up very poor. Ice cream was always a luxury my parents could never afford. I wanted it so badly, but I could never have it. One day when I was established and I had more than enough money to buy my own ice cream, I saw this little boy staring into the ice cream cooler at the corner store. I knew the look on his face too well." He pauses and stares outside at the darkening evening.

"When I asked if his mom or dad was around, he hesitated. You know, like he was afraid to say he was alone because he'd get in trouble. So I said, pick what you want and I'll buy it. The way his eyes lit up when he got that ice cream bar, Colby... I'll never forget that look. And I just want every kid to be able to have ice cream with no questions asked, you know?"

"I'm really happy I get to help you do that, Blaze. It's an honour."

He finishes crunching his cone, and his happy smile returns, as River comes back with Dante.

"You ready? We should get my dad some ice cream on the way home," River says, and takes Blaze's napkin from him over to the garbage.

"Maple Walnut, right?"

"What? No. He's a Strawberry guy. Clearly you've not asked his opinion on maple walnut. Do you two even talk?"

"I guess not." Blaze laughs. "Do I want to know his opinion?"

"He'll tell you it's for old people and he's not old enough for that. Strawberry is what the young girls like so he eats that because it makes him feel young." River rolls his eyes as he heads to the door, and Blaze waves a good bye to us. His happy smile plastered to his face.

"They're so boning each other," Dante blurts once the door is locked behind them.

"D! It's none of your business if they are!" I scold him, but I'm secretly agreeing with him and wondering if the rest of the ranch knows. Blaze never looks at the other ranch hands like he does River, and River hardly ever talks about his dad to us. I've asked many times if I could thank him for his efforts with painting the parts on my counter top, but River always brushes me off.

"You're right." His eyes glitter with mischief. "I have a surprise for you, that's much better than who's boning who gossip."

I raise an eyebrow. "The last time you tried to surprise me I got stung by a bee."

"In my defense I didn't know it was stuck in the flower, okay?"

Calling out to Shelby that we're leaving, we exit through the back door to walk home. The new store location is close enough that I don't need to drive anymore. Dante ditched his old beater car and now he drives mine to the ranch every day. We're still in the same rental place, but we lost Landon as a roommate when he moved to New York for a job.

I'm sad my best friend left, but I'm also happy for Dante and I to officially start a real adult life together. Dan offered him full-time work at the ranch and he loves working with the growing llama herd. When we were teenagers, he thought he'd become a bookkeeper or something similar so he could help with my business.

It's now obvious he has a talent and love for animals. Specifically llamas. He's grown the herd and learned about their fur, and it's added a revenue stream to the ranch. He still works crazy hours depending on what the ranch needs, but together we've been easing into this new life and I couldn't be happier.

"Hey, did Landon text you today? About visiting early September?" Dante asks.

"He did! He said he has tickets for a box suite from a coworker if we really want to visit him." Which I do. I miss him so much and talk to him almost daily. His new job with the farm team of the New York Mafia as one of their strength and conditioning coaches keeps him busy, but he couldn't be happier about it.

The opportunity came to him out of the blue and he jumped on it last year.

"Let's make the plans, then. I love a road trip. Dan will be cool with it."

He unlocks our front door and once inside, he doesn't let me sit, leading me to the bedroom instead.

"Your surprise is sex?"

"Not exactly, but I hope it leads to that." He wiggles his eyebrows and squeezes my ass playfully. "I promise there's no bees this time."

He strips off my clothes and peppers kisses all over as he works to get me naked in record time.

"You know how you like Fun Dip so much?"

"Mmhm." He's licking my neck and he could've asked me if cows were green. I'm not really listening and I'd probably say yes to anything.

"I'm gonna be your personal Lik-a-Stix."

I laugh. "Aren't you already?"

He hastily throws his clothes behind him and pushes me back on the bed.

"Well, maybe, but I don't taste like cherry powder, do I?" He takes a bowl off the nightstand, licks a finger and coats it with powder that he holds out to me. "Lick it."

I use the tip of my tongue to test the powder and it really is a cherry Fun Dip. Holding his finger steady, I work it into my mouth as far as I can go and suck hard.

"Shiittt, Colbs. You're supposed to be the one enjoying this, not me."

I laugh and make him coat his finger with powder again. "I *am* enjoying this. You make a great Lik-a-stix."

I make a show of swirling my tongue around his finger and alternate my suction from hard to soft. Dante is losing his mind and I'm liking this game.

"Lie down," I whisper, and he immediately flops to his back next to me. I lick a path from his belly button to his rib cage and sprinkle powder across the extra saliva I left behind.

His moans and whimpers as I lick all the sugary powder off are more addicting than any kind of candy. I'm as hard as a rock just listening to him.

"You didn't plan to put this on your dick did you?"

He snaps his eyes open. "Maybe?"

"I feel like it might cause hygiene issues."

He shrugs. "Maybe? I'm already close to coming from you sucking on my finger, so I think it's still working out well."

I muffle my laugh in the sheets. Dante has not been afraid to be vocal about what he wants to try or do now that we make the time for each other. And he makes me laugh so much with all his weird and quirky requests. But he's just given me some information I didn't have earlier.

I draw his finger through his own puddle of precum on his belly and swirl it in the powder before shoving it in my mouth.

"Mmm, now that's delicious. Cherry Dante." I repeat the move, but this time I suck his finger slower and stroke his dick in time to my tongue sliding on his finger.

"Jesus fucking Christ, Colbs."

His free hand reaches for my dick and his awkward pulls feel like heaven. This time, I slick his finger with my own fluid and dip it in the bowl. I make a point of forcing Dante to watch me when I put his finger in my mouth, tasting myself and the cherry powder.

"Mmm, that's good too, wanna try it?"

"On your tongue." He croaks and it takes me a minute to understand, but I swipe the sticky fluid from my dick, dip it in the powder and place it on my tongue before offering it to Dante. He licks and sucks at my tongue so hard I fear he might rip it out, and I lean back, smacking around the nightstand for the bottle of lube that's always, ALWAYS, on hand.

Squirting some in my hand, I work his cock how I know he likes it and I suck his finger back in my mouth. His back arches and his free hand reaches for me again and matches my pace.

"Gonna come, Colbs, holy fuck." And he does. Pouring over my fist as he shudders and groans and mutters about how he can never eat cherries again now.

I straddle his thighs and throw my head back, letting him finish me and I moan through my own orgasm. Damn it's never going to get old with him.

I don't even care we're a sticky gooey mess of cherry powder and cum. We can wash up and sheets can be changed.

"Well that didn't go quite as I planned." He laughs.

"I think it went quite well. I found out you like your finger sucked *and* we both taste good with cherries."

He shrugs. "Okay, it's a win-win. For the record, I quite liked being your Lik-a-stix. That was hot."

"It was." I push myself off him and search for something to wipe off with. I throw Dante a towel and head straight for the shower, knowing he'll follow me. As much fun as it was, I can't stand being sticky.

When Dante joins me in the shower, he silently takes the soap and washes me. His work calloused hands send shivers through me, like they always do.

Every day with him is a second chance I never thought I'd have.

Every day of my new life is one I thought I'd never have.

It started with a shy boy and a horse. It grew to a love so big, I didn't think I could contain it.

Now it's everything I can't live without.

Acknowledgments

Every book comes with people I owe a thank you to for helping me get it out to the world. I may have made all the words, but it's a team effort to deliver.

Tammi Hammond, thank you for suggesting the name Lick It Up for Colby's store! One perk of my reader group is participating in my random requests. I needed a name and so many good ones were put out there, but I liked Tammi's the best.

Janet H, we make a great team! Thank you so much for believing in me and badgering me for the next chapters.

Janet M and Jeanette B thank you for the early feedback and the encouragement to keep going.

Thank you, Jen and Sarah for your help to make this the most polished version it can be.

My Naughty List members – oh boy, I owe you all the biggest of thanks. Every one of you showed up with dad jokes and support when life took me by surprise. Your excitement for this book was incredible and I hope it didn't disappoint. I appreciate you all so much!

And you, dear reader! I could never forget you. Without you, there are no words being created. Thank you for reading and I hope we meet again.

Much love,
RM

Also By

If you'd like to read more of my books, scan the QR code with any smart phone to see my back list.

About Author

RM is a Canadian author, wishing winter away one cup of hot chocolate at a time. She believes in big, fluffy love for everyone, unicorns and the perfect cup of coffee. She lives with her supportive husband, rambunctious daughter and a very lazy cat.

If you want to keep in touch, consider joining her newsletter. Sometimes she gives away free stuff just for being a subscriber.

And if you loved the book, please consider leaving a rating or review. If that's not your thing, why not join Neill's Naughty List and talk about it? She loves interacting with readers.

Made in United States
North Haven, CT
18 February 2023